WINNING THE MOUNTAIN MAN'S LOVE

BROTHERS OF SAPPHIRE RANCH
BOOK FIVE

MISTY M. BELLER

Misty M. Beller
BOOKS

Winning the Mountain Man's Love

Cover design by Evelyne Labelle at Carpe Librum Book Design: www.carpelibrumbookdesign.com

ISBN-13 Trade Paperback: 978-1-954810-92-1

ISBN-13 Large Print Paperback: 978-1-954810-93-8

ISBN-13 Casebound Hardback: 978-1-954810-94-5

For I know the thoughts that I think toward you, says the Lord,
thoughts of peace and not of evil, to give you a future and a hope.

Jeremiah 29:11 (NKJV)

CHAPTER 1

March 1870
Silver Dollar, Montana Territory

*J*onah Coulter gripped the stack of posters bearing Patsy's description as he strode down the bustling main street of Silver Dollar, the latest in an endless string of mining towns in this exhausting, fruitless search. After four months of hunting, he was bone-weary, but he'd done almost nothing by way of actually locating little Anna's aunt.

The only real progress he'd made was ruling out women and towns from his list of possible places Patsy of unknown surname could be. Had he really thought he could find a woman in this vast Montana Territory with only her first name and hair color? A fool's delusion.

As he approached the weathered facade of the Silver Dollar Saloon, the raucous laughter spilling from within turned his stomach. Would Patsy frequent this kind of place with her new husband? If so, would she even be a suitable guardian for the seven-year-old girl he'd found in the woods on his family's mountain ranch. But he'd promised to search for Anna's Aunt Patsy and, if she still remained in the Montana Territory, to find her and bring her back. The poor girl's grandmother, who'd been traveling with her, had died, and this aunt was her only remaining family.

Jonah stepped up to the board beside the saloon door, where other notices were posted, and pulled a nail from his satchel. He positioned it so his blow would secure the paper into the wood. Patsy's vague description, penned in his most legible script, stared at him from the topmost sheet. He drew a steadying breath and stepped forward for his task.

A few men drifted from the saloon as he finished nailing the notice. They seemed interested, so he stepped back in case any of them recognized the description.

The pungent aroma of sweat, tobacco, and whisky clouded the fresh air as one of the men murmured something indecipherable to another. They both chuckled.

A third fellow, his dark beard matted enough to hide a small animal, raised a tin cup in salute. "Sounds like a looker. She your'n?"

Jonah gave a hard shake of his head. "My family's taken in her niece. She's the girl's last kin. If any of you know of her, I'd appreciate you pointing me in the right direction."

The man who'd first laughed with his companion gave a toothy grin. "I knew a redhead once. She was a feisty thing."

Jonah raised his brows, a seed of hope planting in his chest. "She still around here?"

The miner shook his head. "Naw. That was back in Indiany. She was the kinda gal who stuck with ya, though."

The guy had the nerve to wink, and Jonah had to clench his jaw to keep from giving the man a lesson about how women should be treated. The men in these towns were all the same. They had no useful information. They just wasted Jonah's time with their crude remarks.

He was ready to move on to the next establishment when the

bearded man spoke up again. "Ya know, I might've seen a gal like that a few months back. She was passing through on a freight wagon, heading west outta town."

Hope tried to break through Jonah's exhaustion. "You're certain? A young woman with red hair?"

The miner scratched his matted beard. "Couldn't miss that fiery mane o' hers. Overheard her telling the driver she was meeting up with her new husband."

New husband. That matched what Anna had said. "Any idea where they were headed?" Jonah worked to keep the desperation from his voice.

The man shrugged. "Sorry, friend. Didn't catch that part. But there's only a couple of towns big enough for settling down in that direction. You might try Sweetwater Springs or Prospect Falls."

Jonah nodded his thanks but felt anything but encouraged.

More towns, more dead ends. But he couldn't return to Anna and his family empty-handed, couldn't fail this last bit of purpose that kept him going.

He tipped his hat to the man. "Much obliged." He turned on his heel and strode away, leaving the men to their vulgar comments.

As Jonah paused outside the town's mercantile to post his next flyer, he gazed out at the mountains rising in the distance, their snow-capped peaks tinted orange by the late afternoon sun. Somewhere out there was a woman who held the key to a little girl's future. And come drought or snowstorm, he aimed to find her.

* * *

May 1870
Missoula Mills, Montana Territory

*P*atience shuffled the deck of cards with practiced ease, the worn edges slipping through her fingers like water over river rocks. The room was thick with cigar smoke and the sharp scent of whiskey, a heady mix that she'd grown accustomed to in her time working at the saloon. Her gaze swept over the players at her table, reading their tells and sizing them up with a gambler's instinct honed by necessity.

One man in particular drew her focus like a lodestone. He hunched over his cards, a scowl etched deep into the lines of his weathered face. The barkeep had pulled her aside when the fellow walked in, warning her in hushed tones to keep a watchful eye on him. *That one's got a temper on him,* he'd muttered. *Liable to blow at any moment, and Lord help whoever's in his path when he does.*

Patience watched him now, noting the pressure coiled in his shoulders, the way his fingers flexed and twitched toward the holster at his hip.

Like a snake preparing to strike.

Slowly, deliberately, she dealt the next hand, keeping her expression carefully neutral even as her heart thumped faster.

She'd seen his type before. He wasn't the cruel sort, the kind who bullied others when they didn't get what they wanted. No, this fellow looked to be one of those men who'd been pushed to the brink by the harsh realities of frontier life. Loss, desperation, the struggle to survive—they could break something inside a person until all that remained was rage. As much as she understood how that could happen, empathized even, she couldn't let his rage put the other patrons at risk.

Each card laid on the table ratcheted up the tension simmering in the air.

The man grew increasingly agitated, muttering curses under his breath as his losses mounted.

Patience maintained her composure, but beneath the table,

her free hand drifted closer to the derringer tucked in the holster hidden under her skirt at her waist. A weapon of last resort, but one she knew how to use if it came to it. Better to defuse his anger before it exploded, if she could manage it.

She dealt the next hand slowly, using the moment to catch his eye. She gave him a smile that disarmed most men. "You seem to be having a rough night." She turned up the charm in her voice. "Perhaps a break would do you good. Clear your head a bit."

His scowl deepened, but he hesitated, his hand hovering over his cards.

She pressed on, keeping her tone pleasant. "I've seen many a man let the cards get the better of him. It's a hard thing to walk away when luck's not on your side. It takes a strong fellow. But from what I've seen, you've got that kind of strength in spades." She let her grin turn lazy, almost like a wink. "Besides, my friend Billy over there behind the counter owes me a favor. Two free rounds for you. On the house."

She held his gaze, watching the struggle play out behind those angry eyes. For a long, strained moment, it looked like his rage might boil over.

She was ready for him to lash out.

But then, slowly, he released a breath and pushed back from the table. "Reckon I'd be a fool to pass up two free drinks."

As he pushed back and tromped toward the bar, she caught Billy's eye and raised two fingers just high enough that he'd see them.

Billy gave a tiny nod. They'd done this several times now. Trouble always came in one form or another. It was her job to stay alert and ready for whatever hand fate dealt her next. Part of her role, anyway. Her other assignment was to increase the house winnings each night. Double them every month—that'd been her promise. Their agreement had been that if she didn't accomplish it in any month, she would go upstairs with the other *girls*.

No matter what, she wouldn't let that happen.

Jackson was a liar, for certain, but so far he'd held up his end of the bargain. She'd first come west after responding to his advertisement in the St. Louis paper for a mail order bride. She'd been desperate to escape her husband's killer and should have taken more time to ask questions.

Not that Jackson would have answered truthfully. He'd paid her fare on the steamboat to Fort Benton, then a wagon ride to Missoula Mills. It wasn't until she met Jackson and entered the saloon with him that she realized his true intentions. He didn't want a wife, he wanted another pretty face for his brothel upstairs.

Never had she done such and never would she. Thankfully, his greed overruled, his stubbornness, and she'd convinced him she could double the profits of his poker room. If she didn't manage it in any given month, she'd agreed to join the other girls.

But she wouldn't. Not if she had breath left in her body. She'd think of something else to stop him.

So far, that hadn't been necessary. She'd accomplished it that first month, then the next, and now she would this month too.

She holstered her derringer with a hand that trembled more than it should, forcing herself to breathe past the tightness in her chest.

She managed a bright grin for the other fellows around the table. "One more hand, then I close the room for an hour. You boys go drum up some grub and meet me back here."

Maybe she shouldn't take this hour off each midday, but she'd be holed up in her dark, smoke-laced room half the night, and she needed a break for decent food and fresh air.

She let Nelson win the final hand, as he needed the cash more than the rest. The lad always sent his winnings back to his widowed mother. She was on track to make the house proceeds she had to for the month.

The men began to disperse, muttering among themselves as they filed out into the main area of the bar.

Best she slip out while she had a chance. After stacking the cards, she headed out the back door. The trading post was only three doors down, and a narrow walkway ran between the buildings so she could leave the alley and enter the store from the front like other customers.

The warm afternoon sun eased her tension as she made her way down the alley, then between the buildings to the board-walk lining the main road through town. A glance through the front windows of the trading post showed the place was busy. She didn't want to face people just now, but she needed to get an order in.

Taking a deep breath, Patience pushed open the door and stepped inside, the tinkling of the bell overhead announcing her arrival.

The proprietor looked up, his eyes crinkling at the corners. "Afternoon, Miss Whitman. What can I do for you?"

Patience returned the smile, hoping it didn't look as forced as it felt. After all the strain in her morning's work, she prefered not have to face people and pretend all was as pleasant as spring in her life. "Just need to place an order. I'll be picking it up tomorrow around this time." After she was paid. She placed her list on the counter, and Mr. Higgins studied the items.

"I'll have that all ready for you in the morning." He lowered the note with a friendly smile. "Anything else I can help you with?"

She shook her head. "Thank you."

As she turned to go, the notice board on the side wall caught her attention. One of the papers fluttered in the breeze that swept in with a customer. She stepped closer, peering at it.

Her breath caught in her throat as she read the words, each one searing into her mind.

Reward: For information about a woman named Patsy, red hair, with a niece named Anna.

Patience's surroundings faded as she stared at the poster, her pulse pounding in her ears.

It couldn't be. How could anyone have found her out here? She'd been so careful, leaving no trace of her past life behind.

The description matched her perfectly, down to the color of her hair. And Anna... Dear, sweet Anna. How did the men who'd killed Michael know about her niece? And why use Hannah's daughter at all?

Where were Hannah and Phillip?

"Is everything all right, Miss Whitman?"

She jumped as Mr. Higgins's concerned voice cut through the fog of her thoughts. "Yes, everything's fine." She jerked away from the notice, but her behavior surely looked odd. Maybe it would be better to confront his suspicion squarely. Surely this man wondered whether she was the woman listed.

She motioned toward the paper. "This seems an odd notice. I'd wonder if they were looking for me"—she patted her high chignon of deep red hair—"except my name isn't Patsy." She gave a conspiratorial smile, then made sure her voice turned casual. "Who posted this, do you know?"

Mr. Higgins's brows furrowed. "A fellow named Jonah Coulter brought it in this morning. He's staying over at the hotel, I hear."

Her heart stuttered at the name. Coulter?

Could that be the man who had killed her husband? If only she'd stuck around the riverboat long enough to find out.

But if this was that cheating scoundrel, how could he have found her so quickly?

She worked to keep her voice steady. "Well, I suppose I should stop and see this Mr. Coulter, just to clear up any confusion. Others might think I'm the one he's looking for."

Higgins nodded, then turned his attention to the next customer in line.

She meandered out of the store, her racing thoughts at odds with her casual step. She had to find out who this Jonah Coulter was and what he wanted with her.

As she walked briskly down the boardwalk toward the hotel, she did her best to calm her frayed nerves. She'd faced worse than this before and come out the other side. She could handle one man, no matter who he was or what he wanted.

But fear coiled in her gut like a snake, ready to strike. She couldn't shake the feeling that her past had caught up with her. That everything she was working so hard to build in this new life was about to come crashing down around her.

Taking a deep breath, Patience straightened her shoulders and quickened her pace.

She wouldn't let that happen. She'd fought too hard and come too far to let anyone take away her future now.

The hotel loomed ahead, its weathered facade casting long shadows in the afternoon sun. Patience paused outside the door, gathering her courage. Then, with a determined set to her shoulders, she pushed inside, ready to face whatever awaited her.

CHAPTER 2

*T*he click of metal on metal jarred Jonah from a restless slumber. His eyes flew open before his mind fully engaged. The dark barrel of a revolver loomed less than an arm's length from his face.

He shifted his focus to the person holding the weapon—and had to blink to get the image clear in his sleep-fogged mind.

A woman. Red hair.

Patsy?

This stop in Missoula was to be his last before trudging back to the ranch. He'd ridden through the night to get here and had been trying to get in a few hours of sleep before he started searching. Could he have found her, here at the very end?

When she spoke, her voice came out hard. "Jonah Coulter?"

"Yes, ma'am." He managed to squeeze out the words.

"I've got questions for you. And you'd best answer them straight."

Jonah swallowed, his mouth dry as sawdust. The woman's grip on the gun was steady, practiced. She meant business. No trace of feminine softness here.

"Happy to answer." But he'd rather not do it lying flat on his back. He started to edge up to sitting in bed. "You can put that thing down."

When he moved, she shifted the barrel to aim at his face. "Stay where you are." Her tone left little doubt that she'd pull the trigger.

He halted, still on his back, though his head rested farther up on his pillow. "I promise I mean you no harm." Especially if this was Patsy. He'd be protecting her, not hurting her.

"Are you the one putting up the flyers?" Her face gave no hint of any emotion except anger.

"If you mean the ones looking for a woman named Patsy, then yes."

"What do you want with her?"

He raised his brows. "Is your name Patsy?"

"No." The response came short and swift, like a punch to the gut.

His hope sank. She had to be Anna's aunt. She fit the vague description—age and hair color mostly. And she had the same rounded cherub cheeks as the little girl. Why would this woman trust him so little that she'd lie?

She must be in some kind of trouble.

Before he could find a way to ask, she spoke again. "Name's Patience Whitman."

Ah.

Patience. Patsy could certainly be a nickname. He'd been searching for women with all the names that could be derived from Patsy—Patricia, Patrice, Pasquale, Patty. But he'd never thought of Patience.

He needed to tread carefully. He'd seen mountain cats with less searing stares. "It's nice to meet you, Mrs. Whitman. Do you, by chance, have a niece named Anna? She's seven years old with medium brown hair. She was traveling with her grandmother to find you."

The woman's eyes widened for a half a heartbeat. She must

not have known about their search. Anna hadn't been certain whether she did or not.

When she didn't say anything, Jonah added, "She calls her grandmother Gamma."

"How do you know about Anna?" Patsy—and he was certain that was who this was—glared, her head turning a little so she could stare more through her right eye. "You'd best start explaining yourself. My finger's getting twitchy on this trigger."

He'd have to tell her everything. Every part of the story he knew, anyway. He had a feeling this conversation was about to get a whole lot more complicated, but for the sake of the little girl waiting for word of her aunt, he had to try.

Even if it killed him. Which, considering the gun still aimed at his face, it just might.

He took a deep breath to steady his nerves. "My brothers and I live on a ranch in the mountains. We found Anna and her grandmother." He raised his brows. "Your mother, maybe?" She gave no answer, so he kept going. "They camped on my family's ranch last winter. The snow got thick and the weather miserable. We brought them in our house, and my sister-in-law—she's a doctor—treated them for cold exposure. Anna was fine, but her grandmother was already mostly unconscious."

He swallowed hard. He'd really not wanted to break the news this way, but this woman seemed to need every little detail to convince herself of his honesty. "Sadly, she passed on that evening. Anna's been with us ever since. She told us about her aunt, whom she and her grandmother were traveling to see. She didn't know the particulars, not even the aunt's last name. Only that the lady had come to the Montana Territory to be married."

The gun wobbled a tiny bit when he spoke those last words, and she tightened her jaw. "Why isn't Anna with her parents? Where are they in all this?" Her pitch came out sharp, accusatory, as if she already suspected the answer but needed to hear it confirmed aloud.

Jonah hated to say. Even a woman as hardened as this one shouldn't have to be told like this that her entire family was dead. That the bright-eyed little girl who shared her blood was now an orphan, adrift in a world that had already been so cruel to her.

But he had no choice. Mrs. Whitman deserved the truth, no matter how painful it might be.

"I'm sorry." He kept his voice gentle. "From what Anna's told us, her parents passed away. I think her grandfather has been gone a while, so it was just her and her grandmother. It sounds like they were settled well before they came west. But now..." He trailed off, letting the unspoken implication hang in the air between them. He couldn't help but add, "I'm sorry, Mrs. Whitman."

She visibly swallowed, and the gun trembled again. "It's Miss. I'm not married." The words came out in a hoarse whisper, almost like a side note as she took in the massive load he'd just handed her.

He could ask what happened to her marriage later—or not, as it might not be any of his business. For now, he had to help her face this awful truth. His own chest ached. Despite the gun she still aimed at him, he wished he could make this easier on her. Not that there could be any comfort for the grief that came from so much loss.

A single tear tracked down her cheek, glistening in the dim light of the hotel room.

But her expression still held strength. And determination. "How do I know you're telling the truth?" Though her voice was still wary, a note of desperation crept in. "How do I know this isn't a trick?"

Jonah met her gaze steadily. "How would I know anything about your family? And why would I lie? I'm here because Anna needs you. You're the only family she has left." He wanted to ask what kind of trouble she was in that would make her so suspicious, but that would likely put her even more on guard.

She drew a shaky breath, squaring her shoulders as if steeling herself from the weight of her emotions.

He had to speak before she made up her mind against him. "Is there anything I can do to prove I'm telling the truth? Your niece and mother didn't have much with them when we found them. A few brightly colored blankets. It seemed your mother liked bright colors. She wore a necklace that Anna has now. Big round beads. Lots of different colors."

Patsy straightened. "What are the beads made of?"

She was testing him.

He worked to recall as much as he could, though it'd been months since he'd been home, and he hadn't paid much attention. "They're wooden. I think smaller near the clasp and larger near the center of the necklace." He could hold up his fingers to show the size, but she didn't look ready for him to move just yet.

She narrowed her gaze, making him think his description had made her more wary, not less. "Michael told you about the necklace, didn't he? It's not worth much, I can tell you that."

He let his confusion show. "I don't know who Michael is. I know about the necklace because Anna wears it all the time."

Miss Whitman straightened her shoulders, her jaw set with determination as she stepped back. "I'm leaving now." Her voice had once again turned hard and unyielding. "You'd best get out of town today. The next time I see you. I'll shoot first and not waste time with questions."

As she backed out the door, disappointment soured his belly. How had he not convinced her? The truth was on his side, yet he'd failed to make her believe him.

Light from the hallway glimmered in her red hair as she stepped from the room and pulled the door closed.

The click of the door latch fired like a gunshot in the quiet room, releasing Jonah from the hold of his covers. He surged to his feet and started pulling on his clothes. Should he go find Miss Whitman and try to convince her again? Maybe if he brought Chuck from the livery, or someone else she might know around town to stand as a character witness for him.

She was so skittish, though, he had a feeling he needed to find a way to prove his claim—something she wouldn't be able to deny.

Should he bring Anna here?

Even as the thought rose, he pushed it down.

He didn't like the thought of bringing a child to such a harsh place as a mining town. The journey alone would be hard—two days here and back if he went slower for the girl. They'd have to sleep on the hard ground. Even if he decided to do it, Jericho wouldn't hear of her leaving the ranch, and Naomi and Eric would be on his side. They were so protective of the girl, not allowing anything that might make her feel insecure or afraid, as she'd been when she was stranded in the snow and cold, her grandmother too sick to help.

No. He wouldn't try to bring Anna here.

But could he fetch the necklace?

If he could get it from the ranch and present it to Patsy, would she consider it proof enough? It would certainly prove that Michael—whoever he was—hadn't told Jonah about the piece.

Making a decision, he finished dressing and grabbed up the few belongings he'd pulled from his saddle bags. He'd ride back to the ranch to get the necklace—that would work, surely—and maybe he would raise the idea of bringing Anna herself.

At the very least, maybe someone else would want to come back with him and talk to Patsy. Getting Anna's aunt to come see her wasn't Jonah's responsibility alone anyway. He'd taken on the job of finding her so he'd have something to keep him away from the ranch while Naomi and Eric set up their new life. His ex-fiancée and her new husband...

He still wasn't ready to deal with that.

Well, at least he'd found Anna's aunt, though obviously he wasn't going to be able to talk her into doing right by her niece. He never had been good at getting a woman to choose him. At least not when she wasn't backed into a corner.

* * *

*P*atience had to stay calm. In control. Telling herself that wasn't helping, though.

Her hands trembled as she closed the door to the small room above the cafe she shared with Lottie.

Surely the man who called himself Jonah was lying. Her entire family couldn't be lost to her.

But how would he know about Anna? The necklace?

Was her niece truly alone in the world?

Lottie looked up from the washbasin, a smile brightening her eyes. It dimmed when she saw Patience.

They'd only managed to get such private quarters because Lottie cooked in the cafe, and Patience had come to appreciate the older woman's company as much as the narrow chamber they shared.

Lottie's brows drew together. "What's wrong, dear? You look like you've seen a ghost."

Was she that transparent? She tried for a smile. Lottie was the one person she could talk to, the one person who didn't judge her for her occupation or how she spent her time. Patience hadn't shared much about her past with the woman, only that she was a widow, a situation they had in common.

But Lottie's husband had died of a weak heart. He hadn't been murdered by a slick card shark. That part of the story, Patience hadn't told her.

Lottie dried her hands on her apron and reached for her, tugging her to one of the chairs around their small table, cast-offs from the business below. They'd repaired the broken legs but couldn't do anything for the scarred wood.

Patience sank into the seat, and Lottie settled in the other, looking her up and down. "Well, go on then. What happened?"

Where should she start? With the part that ached the most, maybe.

She swallowed. "I found out there's a man looking for me. He says his family found my niece. That...the rest of my kin are all...gone." Her voice cracked as she forced out the words.

Lottie covered Patience's hands with her own. "Oh, honey. No."

The gentle answer released a geyser in her chest, and a sob rose up against her control. Tears spilled down her cheeks. Mama. She couldn't be gone. Not yet.

As soon as she had enough money saved to buy the house and land, she'd planned to write her mother, to invite her out if she dared venture away from Father's oppressive hold. It turned out she hadn't been bound by his rules for a while now.

Another sob ventured, though this time she couldn't name its cause. She certainly wasn't crying over her father's death. Hannah maybe. How could she and Phillip both be gone? What could have possibly taken every blood relation Patience had? Every person she could call family?

Except Anna. She sucked in a breath, doing everything she could to stop the tumult spewing from her. Another deep breath cleared her mind enough that she could speak her concern. "I don't know if it's true. I'm not sure I can trust this man."

Lottie's brow furrowed. "Why wouldn't you believe him? What reason would he have to lie?"

Because the man who killed my husband might have come after me.

The words lodged in Patience's throat. She desperately

wanted to unburden herself to Lottie, but fear held her back. Not fear of what Lottie would think. Not really.

If her husband's murderer or his cronies ever followed her trail, the last thing she wanted was to put Lottie in danger by giving her too much information.

"I just...I need to be sure," Patience said instead, forcing herself to meet Lottie's concerned gaze. "Before I upend my life again chasing shadows and rumors."

Lottie leaned forward, her expression intense. "Patience, listen to me. If there is even a chance your niece is out there, scared and alone, you need to go to her. That innocent child needs her kin."

Lottie's words cut through the haze of Patience's spiraling thoughts. She was right. It didn't matter if Jonah wasn't telling the whole truth.

What mattered was Anna.

If her dear little niece had ended up in these mountains somehow, Patience had to find her. She had to bring her home —whatever home looked like now—and care for the poor child. The thought of Anna going through such trauma sent a shiver down Patience's spine.

She managed a nod and another deep breath. "You're right."

Lottie pulled her into a hug, and she allowed herself to be comforted. Then she stood and wiped her eyes. She only had a few more minutes before she had to get back to the saloon.

As Lottie moved back to her washbasin, Patience stepped to the trunk that held all her belongings. She had to dig past blankets and a few garments that were too nice to wear in this rough town. Finally, her fingers closed on the small, cloth-bound journal.

She pulled it out and rested it in her lap. The cover had frayed at the corners, but the lace trim remained intact, if yellowed with age. Her father had given it to her when she turned eight, one of the few gifts he'd ever bestowed that seemed just for her.

It had been so special, the journal itself so lovely, that she never dared mar the pristine pages with her scrawling hand and silly thoughts.

Patience ran her fingers over the cover, her throat tight. She'd always hoped that someday, she'd find the courage to face her father and mend the rift between them. That she'd be able to show him she'd made something of herself, despite his doubts and criticisms.

Now that chance had slipped away. Her father was gone, taking with him any hope of reconciliation. Tears blurred her vision as she clutched the journal to her chest, mourning not only the loss of her family but the unwritten words that would forever remain unsaid.

She opened the front cover and pulled out the piece of canvas, stiff from being pressed in this book for so many years. As she stared at the image painted on it, that familiar longing swelled in her chest. The white cottage, the wide green valley with a stream running through it. Indiana. One day she would own a cottage just like this, in a valley every bit this lovely. She would find this place in Indiana and build her own life. Free from anyone who could control her—especially a man.

She was closer than she'd ever been before. Manning the poker room for Jackson paid well, and she'd been saving every penny.

But if she took Anna in, how much longer would she have to wait until she had enough to build this image for herself? She blinked to clear that question away, slipped the canvas back in the book, then closed the cover.

CHAPTER 3

*J*onah opened the saloon door, and a rush of stale, smoky air met his nose. Still, he stepped inside, his brother at his heels. Maybe bringing Sampson back with him when he'd gone to the ranch to retrieve Anna's necklace had been a mistake. Sampson was the second to youngest—barely a man—but he'd been hankering to get off the ranch a few days, so Jonah had agreed. But he'd not expected to bring him straight into this saloon.

He'd gone to the hotel first when they arrived back in Missoula Mills, but the clerk said Miss Whitman worked at Jackson's saloon.

The idea churned in his belly.

During all those months he'd searched, he'd thought about every possible situation Anna's aunt could be in. Saloon girl or brothel worker had certainly been on the list. But deep down, he'd not actually believed a woman related to sweet Anna would succumb to that kind of life.

He scanned the dim interior as he kept his breathing shallow against the stench. Since dusk had fallen, the place was filling up. Plenty of miners ready to spend their small earnings lined the bar and the tables in the middle of the floor.

To the left, a rowdy cluster of men gathered around a larger poker table, their voices rising and falling with each turn of the cards.

A flash of red caught his focus, and he homed in on the spot.

Miss Whitman, her hair piled in a becoming mass of curls. She held a hand of cards, just like the others. He couldn't help but stare. Was this how she spent her free time? Gambling? Or was she drumming up business for…her work?

He started forward, his boots thumping on the wooden floorboards.

Sampson trailed close behind him. Maybe he should have insisted he stay outside, but it might help to have his brother at his back. And besides, Sampson might be a little naive, the way Jericho had kept them all on the ranch these past years. It would be good for him to see the ways of the world. The ugly side. To know how truly distasteful getting mixed up in this lot could be.

They were halfway to the table when a shout sounded. One of the men across from Miss Whitman leapt to his feet. Light from the chandelier flashed on metal in his hand. A pistol.

The barrel was aimed straight at Anna's aunt.

"You cheatin' little—" The man's shout slurred, but his words were discernable even across the tables between them.

Jonah didn't wait for the rest. His rifle was in his hands before he even realized he'd drawn it, the stock solid against his shoulder. "Put the gun down." He spoke loudly enough to be heard above the voices, not that anybody was talking now. He leveled his tone, lacing it with steel as solid as the lead bullet in his Winchester. "Put the gun down and walk away."

The man looked over at Jonah, his eyes fierce and his nostrils flaring. He still kept his revolver aimed at Miss Whitman. Then he darted a wild glance toward the woman. For a moment, it looked like he might actually pull the trigger.

Jonah spoke a little louder. "You shoot and your body will fall before hers. My rifle carries a lot more power than that handgun. She'll be fine in a week, but your carcass'll be buried outside of town tomorrow. Or picked clean by vultures tonight."

The tension in the man's shoulders eased a touch.

Jonah gave him an out. "Drop the gun and you can walk out with your head high."

The man's eyes darted between Jonah and Miss Whitman. His hand wavered slightly, the muzzle of the revolver dipping.

For a long, tense moment, nobody in the saloon moved or spoke.

Then, with a muttered curse, the man lowered his gun and tossed it onto the poker table with a clatter. He raised both hands, palms out. "I'm done here anyway." He shot a venomous glare at Miss Whitman before turning on his heel and stalking toward the exit.

As he passed by Jonah, he slowed and sent a hateful leer. "You'll regret the day you ever stuck your nose in someone else's business, boy." Then he strode the final distance to the door and slammed it behind him.

Jonah let out a slow breath, lowering his rifle. Only now did he realize that Sampson had moved along the windows to a position where he'd been behind that scoundrel, his revolver in hand. He gave his brother a nod, and Sampson tucked the gun back in his waistband.

The saloon remained eerily quiet, the patrons shifting their gazes between him and Miss Whitman, who sat perfectly poised, her expression unruffled as if she hadn't just had a gun pointed at her heart.

With a smile, she passed the deck of cards to the man on her right. "If you gentlemen will excuse me a moment, I have some business to attend to. Please, continue playing, and I shall return shortly." Her voice was smooth as honey, her smile dazzling.

The spell broke, and the men mumbled their assent, some casting curious glances at Jonah as they picked up their cards.

Miss Whitman rose and glided toward Jonah, her skirts swishing. She stopped in front of him, looking him up and down with an appraising eye. "Well now, it appears chivalry is not entirely dead after all. Though I daresay I had the situation well in hand." Her green eyes sparkled with amusement tinged with...annoyance?

Not exactly the reaction he'd expected from a woman who'd just been threatened at gunpoint. Where was her fear? "I brought the necklace. To show you I'm telling the truth about Anna."

At the mention of her niece's name, Miss Whitman's playful expression faltered. Real emotion flashed in her eyes before she shuttered it away. "I see. Well then, let us discuss this matter somewhere more private, shall we?"

She turned and headed toward the back of the saloon, not waiting to see if Jonah and Sampson followed. They had little choice but to trail after her, weaving between tables. She led them through a door into a hallway, then outside to the alley behind the building.

The cool night air offered a welcome respite from the smoky saloon. Miss Whitman turned to face them, arms crossed. Gone was the flirtatious poker dealer. This was a woman who knew her own mind and would not be cowed.

Anger simmered in her stance, her eyes flashing with a defiant fire. "I had it under control in there. If you had let me handle him, I could have smoothed things over so he didn't leave bearing a grudge."

Jonah flinched. The woman didn't offer even a hint of gratitude after he'd risked his life to save her. "How exactly would you have done that?" He wanted to cross his arms to match her stance, but he would keep his cool.

"I've been dealing with men like Douglas for years." She

dropped her hands, blowing out a breath as if he'd frustrated her. "What's done is done now. Show me this supposed proof."

Jonah bit back a retort and shoved his hand into his coat pocket to pull out the necklace. She had a lot of nerve being irritated with him after all the work he'd gone through to find her, to prove he was telling the truth, and then to save her sorry behind, not to mention his family was keeping her niece safe while she sat here whiling away her life playing poker.

He didn't say any of that though, just pulled out the necklace. It glinted in the moonlight as he held it out to her. "Your mother was wearing it when we found her and your niece."

Miss Whitman's eyes widened, the toughness falling away from her like the dried shell from a pecan. She reached for the string of beads, then cradled it in her palms. "My mother treasured this. Her mother-in-law gave it to her when she and my father were married."

She looked up at him then, her eyes shimmering. She didn't seem to know what to say.

"Will you come with us to Anna now?"

She hesitated, conflict warring in her eyes. Did she still not believe him? Or did something else hold her back? Regrets maybe? He could well imagine so, but surely not so much that they would separate her from family. Not anything that she would hold against an innocent little girl.

Then, with a shaky breath, she nodded. "I'll come. But I...I need to work out some things first. I'll meet you at the hotel at noon tomorrow."

Relief washed through him. "Thank you. I'll have a horse for you." A thought slipped in. "Or would you rather a wagon?" Maybe she didn't know how to ride. Though if that was the case, she'd better learn the skill soon if she was to survive in these parts.

She shook her head. "A horse is fine." Then she took a step

backward, toward the door to the saloon. "Good night, Mr. Coulter."

Before he could answer with the same, she disappeared through the doorway, closing it solidly behind her. He let out a long exhale. He'd done it. Two days from now, he'd have Miss Whitman to the ranch and reunited with her niece.

He turned toward the hotel, but realization stopped him dead. Sampson. Where had his brother gone in all the chaos?

* * *

*P*atience stepped inside the saloon the next morning, her boots clicking against the worn wooden floorboards, breaking the stillness as she made her way to the bar. Her chest had turned to lead with the weight of the decision she had to make.

Should she bring Anna back here to Missoula Mills, where she already had lodging and a well-paying job? Or set off with her niece to find the home Patience had always dreamed of?

A little white cottage nestled in a wide valley with a creek running through. When she'd found the little painting in a curiosity shop when she was a girl, it had been labeled with a tiny gold plaque that read *Indiana*. That meant there must be a stretch of land in Indiana that looked just like that painting. Hopefully many such places. She would have the cottage built, if needed. Yet the peace that painting exuded…would she find the peace when she re-created the scene?

She didn't know. She only knew she had to choose her path now, for that decision would determine what she told Mr. Jackson in just a few short minutes. He wouldn't be happy to see her leave, but she'd paid her dues the last two months, more than earning back the money he'd put out for her transportation to Missoula Mills. Money she'd allowed him to pay under false pretenses, the weasel.

She wouldn't make the mistake of underestimating him again. She couldn't give him the upper hand. Maybe it was best she cut ties completely. But she only had half the money she'd need to buy that property. She'd checked on the cost of land as she traveled upriver on her way to Missoula Mills. Plus she'd need funds to build the house.

Behind the counter, Billy looked up from the glass he was polishing, his weathered face creasing into a smile. "Mornin', Miss Patience. You're here early."

She forced a smile. "Is Mr. Jackson here yet?"

The bartender's eyes clouded at their employer's name. "Back in his office, last I saw." Though Billy was tall and broad enough to make most men cower, even he knew it was better to steer a wide berth around Jackson.

She should march to his office and get the conversation over with. But maybe she needed another minute to gather her strength—and courage. She settled on one of the stools at the bar.

He studied her as he wiped another glass with his beefy hands, then placed it in the slot where he could quickly grab it tonight and moved to the next. "Somethin' weighin' on your mind?"

She sighed. "I'm trying to decide if I should leave Missoula Mills for good."

Billy's eyebrows shot up. "Leave? Where would you go?"

She took a folded towel and the next glass to be dried. "I just found out my sister and her husband died. Left a little girl behind—my niece Anna. She was staying with my mother, but now Mama's passed too. I'm going to go bring my niece to live with me."

"I'm sorry to hear that." The tenor of Billy's voice dropped. He set the cup and rag down, giving her his full attention. "What's holdin' you back?"

How could she explain her reluctance? She should be eager

to put this place behind her. "I've got a good thing going here. Money coming in steady. If I leave..." She shook her head. "It'll be harder to provide for a child. Especially if I give up the gambling."

Billy considered her words. Finally, he spoke, his voice gentle but firm. "Miss Patience, you're one of the sharpest poker players I've ever seen. But just 'cause you're good at something don't mean it's where you belong forever."

Her gaze drifted to the empty poker tables, the green felt worn and faded. How many nights had she spent there, building a reputation, gaining respect? But now, with Anna waiting for her, everything felt different. Was this life too dangerous for a child?

"You think I should go for good? Leave all this behind?" It felt scary, starting over again. Even though she wanted desperately to finally start building her new life. But...leaving something she knew she could do well...

Billy's gaze held steady. "Miss Patience, if anyone can make a fresh start, it's you. You've got grit and smarts in spades. Don't let fear hold you back from reaching for something better."

He rubbed another glass dry. "And forgive me for being forward, but this ain't no life for a lady. Especially not one raising a little girl." He gestured around at the empty saloon, his focus shifting to the poker table she usually manned.

Then he met her gaze again. "You gotta leave it behind. Find that fresh start you been dreamin' about." The lines at the corners of his eyes creased.

The image of her dream slipped through her mind. Rich green grass. A pretty white house with curtains in the windows she'd sewn herself. It would be a while before she made it happen, though. She'd have to fight hardscrabble to earn the rest of what she'd need.

Billy's gaze homed on her, his head tilting. "You said your

mama just passed. Is there...? Would there be any kind of inheritance?"

The question hung in the air, raising memories of the last time she had seen her father. He'd refused to look at her. Just kept his nose in the morning paper, pretending she didn't exist at all. Fresh hurt burned her throat.

She brought her focus back to reality. She wrinkled her nose to lighten the tension in her tone. "I wouldn't bet on it." The irony of her words slipped in, considering her current profession.

But even as the words left her lips, a new thought slipped in. "Although..." She worked the notion through all the possible reasons it might not be true. "He would have left his estate to Mama. If I'm one of her last two living relatives..." Her and Anna. Patience wouldn't touch Anna's portion, but unless her father's business had taken a sharp decline... Even half of the estate would be more than enough to buy land and build a house, and there'd be plenty to set aside to live on for years.

Hope flickered in her chest, small but stubborn.

"There you go. Seems to me the answer is clear." Billy patted her hand. "You gotta go get that little girl. Bring her someplace safe and green where she can grow up proper."

She blinked back the sudden sting of tears. "Thank you, Billy. You're a wise old soul, you know that?" She squeezed his hand, and his cheeks reddened above his thick whiskers. She rose from the stool. "I'm gonna tell Jackson I'm leaving today. He won't like it, but that's too bad." Her jaw firmed as she started toward the hall. "Wish me luck."

"You don't need luck. You got gumption and then some. Go on and give Jackson a piece of your mind." He winked. "I'll be here if you need backup."

Patience took a deep breath, squaring her shoulders. She would give her notice, collect her pay, and set her eyes on that distant horizon—on home.

Her and Anna's bright new beginning.

CHAPTER 4

*J*onah glanced back at Missoula Mills, the town disappearing behind a veil of pine trees as he and Miss Whitman rode away. The gelding he'd bought for her fell into an easy cadence beside his own horse, her scant luggage tied securely to the saddle.

Had he been right to leave Sampson behind? His brother had been eager to teach two men who wanted to learn sluice mining. Both fellows were men he'd met in the saloon while Jonah was outside talking with Miss Whitman, but they seemed like decent folks. Sampson had promised to return to the ranch as soon as he finished his instruction—a week or two at most.

Sampson, like Jonah and the rest of their brothers, knew sluice mining like the lines on their callused hands. It was the method they'd first used to mine the sapphires on their ranch. The sapphires they were supposed to keep secret. Jericho was determined not to let word of the gems spread so they didn't get unwanted visitors on the ranch.

Still, a niggle of doubt lingered. Jericho wouldn't like Jonah coming back without Sampson. The oldest brother had always been so protective of their land and kin. He feared strangers getting too close, learning about the sapphires. Part of it probably stemmed from a deep-seated dread that one of them would run off and join a rowdy mining camp, just like their Lucy had done all those years ago.

Lucy. She'd been the oldest—two years older than Jericho—and she'd been wonderful. The only person who'd ever really understood Jonah. The only person who saw him as more than second-best, an option only if nobody better could be found.

"Tell me about your family." Miss Whitman's voice pulled him from those less-than-happy thoughts. "Who else lives on this ranch of yours?"

Jonah cleared his throat. Where to start? "Well. There's Jericho, my older brother. He's head of the family, and he's married to Dinah. She worked as a doctor before she and her sister came west. We put her talent to use often enough, though." He almost snorted. He'd given her one of her toughest cases, having been run over by a wagon wheel the first hour the sisters had arrived on the ranch. Dinah had stopped him from bleeding out there on the hillside and managed to set the bone so he barely had a limp now. He'd known men who broke their thigh bones like he had and now could barely walk because of the way the doctor had set the limb. Dinah possessed talent, no doubt about it.

Miss Whitman watched him, clearly waiting for him to go on.

He might as well list them in order of age. "Then there's me, the second oldest. Then Jude and his wife, Angela. They built a cabin just down the slope from the main house. Then Gilead and Sampson, who was there with me in Missoula Mills. And Miles is the baby."

Jonah couldn't help the grin that twitched his cheeks. "He wouldn't like to be called that, of course. He's seventeen."

Miss Whitman's expression eased into a smile that made her look even prettier than when he'd first seen her at the livery as they were preparing to set out. Even then, he'd been surprised how different she looked than in the saloon. Not as hardened. More like…a lady.

Now she looked even softer as she said, "I'll bet not."

Once more his chest pinched. "We had an older sister, Lucy. She passed a couple years ago, and now my niece and nephew live with us. Lillian and Sean."

Her brows rose. "Are they close to Anna's age?"

He tipped his head. "Lillian is twelve, I think, and Sean is eight." They grew so fast, it was hard to keep up sometimes.

Miss Whitman turned her focus back to the road. "And Anna is almost eight." Her voice sounded wistful, like she wasn't talking to him at all.

"Dinah's sister and her husband live nearby. They built a cabin in a little clearing a few minutes' walk from the main house. They have a daughter who's almost two, and Anna's been staying with them."

Miss Whitman's gaze jerked to him. "She's not living with your family? Do you know these people well? Is she safe there?"

"Yes, ma'am." At the worry in her expression, Jonah added a nod. "Eric and Naomi are good people. Some of the best I know. Anna couldn't be in better hands."

Her shoulders relaxed a fraction, but the crease between her brows remained. "What kind of man is this Eric? Does he have a temper?"

"He's a good man, Patsy, I prom—" He stopped short the moment he heard her given name slip out of his mouth. Or rather, her nickname. He dipped his chin in apology. "I'm sorry, Miss Whitman."

She gave a quick shake of her head. "I don't care what you call me. What of this man my niece is living with? Does he have a temper? Is he controlling?"

She didn't care what he called her? He'd have to revisit that thought later.

"Not at all. He's steady as a rock." He might not have said the same when Eric first came. They'd clashed a few times over Naomi. But Eric had proved himself to be the man Naomi thought him. The more Jonah had gotten to know Eric, the more he'd come to respect him. Admire him, even. "He's a hard worker, and honest to a fault. You don't have to worry about Anna with him and Naomi."

The tightness around Patsy's eyes betrayed her lingering concerns. "And...is she happy there? With them?"

The vulnerability in her voice tightened his chest. He chose his next words carefully. "It took some time, but yes, she's doing well now. Her and Mary Ellen—that's Eric and Naomi's little girl—are thick as thieves. Like sisters, really. And Naomi and Eric love her like she's their own."

Something flashed across Patsy's face. Hurt, maybe. Or regret.

He shouldn't have made it sound like Anna didn't need her blood kin. "She talks about her Gamma all the time," he added quickly. "And she's been counting down the days until she gets to see her aunt again. Just you wait. She'll be bouncing with excitement when we ride into the yard."

Though Patsy kept her gaze fixed ahead, a ghost of a smile curved her lips. "I've missed her too. So much. I just...I hope she remembers me."

"Of course she will. You're her family." Jonah studied Patsy's profile. So different from the fierce, confident woman who had held him at gunpoint during their first meeting, or the shrewd gambler who'd headed a poker table full of raucous men. Now, she seemed fragile somehow, breakable, as if she truly feared her niece might not want her. "Have you thought about what you'll do? After we reach the ranch?"

She sighed, the sound heavy. "I need to get to know Anna again and give her the chance to get to know me. It's been so long. Five years..." She trailed off.

He didn't prompt her, just waited. They had plenty of time to talk. No sense rushing her if she was feeling melancholy.

After a few moments, Patsy went on. "I won't impose on your family though. I'll stay just long enough for Anna to get used to me. A few days at most. Then we'll head to Fort Benton and onward to start a new life."

"You won't be imposing." The words rushed out. "We've got plenty of room, and everyone will be glad to have you stay. Anna's our family now, which makes you family too."

Patsy's expression shuttered, her poker face sliding into place like armor. Unreadable. Closed off.

He must have said something wrong. But what? Maybe he'd been too forward calling her family.

Maybe he could get her talking again with a question or two. "And then what will you do?"

She shrugged. "I have plans."

He waited for her to continue, but she merely focused on the road, spine straight as a ruler. Gone was the easy camaraderie of moments before.

He turned back to the trail as well, the clop of the horses' hooves and the creak of saddle leather filling the silence between them. The rugged Montana landscape stretched out before them, stunning and mysterious. Much like the woman riding beside him.

He'd thought he had her figured out—the clever card sharp, the protective aunt, the determined survivor. But Patsy Whitman kept surprising him, revealing new facets like a finely cut sapphire. Glimpses of vulnerability, flashes of warmth, all tucked behind that unreadable mask she wore so well.

What secrets lay behind those forest-green eyes?

She was a mystery, this woman. One he found himself desperately wanting to unravel.

* * *

*J*onah prodded the log with a stick, coaxing the flames to life in their campfire as the sun dipped behind the mountains. Not even the bright oranges and pinks of the sunset could lighten his mood tonight. Was it only leaving Sampson behind in Missoula Mills that gnawed at him? His little brother was more than capable, but what would Jericho say when Jonah showed up without him?

He glanced over at Miss Whitman's bedroll, neatly arranged a respectable distance from his own. She'd hardly said two words to him all afternoon on the trail, her usual quick wit and charm notably absent. He'd expected at least a few questions about her niece Anna, but every time he'd looked at her as they rode that day, her green eyes had stared into the distance.

The fire crackled and popped as Jonah added another log. He almost had enough flame to heat water for a stew—once Miss Whitman returned with a pot full from the creek. It'd been nearly ten minutes since she'd walked away in that blue dress, his old metal pot swinging at her side. Good thing she hadn't turned around to check on him and caught him watching because... Well, because that blue dress drew a man's eye.

He shifted the last log, then pushed to his feet. He should make sure the horses' ropes were secure before full dark settled.

A piercing scream shattered the quiet. His pulse surged and he spun the direction it had come from. The creek. He sprinted that way, weaving through the trees.

Had she seen a snake? A bear? A mountain lion? Any could be out this late in the spring.

Blast. He'd forgotten to grab his rifle. He had his hunting knife, but that would do little against a bear. He was nearly there, though. He'd need to find out the trouble and go back for his gun if he had to.

When he could see the waterline through the trees ahead, a moving figure made his heart catch in his throat.

Two figures.

Patsy stood knee-deep in the water, struggling against a man whose hands gripped her shoulders, pushing her down.

"Stop!" Jonah bellowed the word as he lunged the last step to the bank and leaped into the icy water.

When Jonah reached them, he launched himself at the man with a roar, slamming them both crashing into the creek.

As they wrestled on their knees in the water, he wrapped his arms around the man's torso, pinning his arms to his side. The rogue thrashed and struggled, his elbow slamming into Jonah's ribs.

Pain exploded in his side, but he didn't let up his hold. He was bigger than this guy, and he wasn't about to let him go.

Out of the corner of his eye, he saw Patsy stumble back, but she froze at the water's edge and watched. What was she doing?

He shouted, "Run!"

His momentary distraction gave the scoundrel the upper hand, and he flipped Jonah on his back, plunging his face under water.

Jonah caught his first clear look at the man's face. Black hair slicked back against his head. Thick beard. Plenty of lines on his face. A face Jonah had seen before.

It was that cheating gambler who'd pulled a gun on Patsy in the saloon.

Fury surged through him. He tucked his body into a ball, dropped his feet to the ground, and propelled himself off the sandy creek bed into the guy, who staggered backward in the knee-high water.

A flash of blue fabric made Jonah's blood run cold. Why hadn't Patsy run?

She stood behind the fellow, the metal pot raised. With a cry, she swung for the man's head.

He must have seen Jonah's reaction, for he spun just in time to protect his skull.

The pot hit his arm instead, knocking him to his knees. He let out a howl, gripping his elbow.

Patsy raised the pot to strike again, but Jonah struggled to his feet. He had to get her out of the mix.

Before he could get close enough to attack, Patsy brought her weapon down for a second time. Their attacker saw it coming and grabbed the metal edge. Using the force of Patsy's blow, he sent her flying across the stream into deeper water, the pot slipping from her grasp.

The blackguard had a weapon now. He turned to face Jonah.

But Jonah had a weapon too.

He reached into his belt and unsheathed his knife.

The scoundrel spun and dashed into the woods.

Jonah charged after him, but dry ground gave the man too much advantage. He sprinted through the trees, disappearing within seconds into the darkness.

Breathing heavily, Jonah gave up the chase, unwilling to leave Patsy on her own again.

Had the man been alone, or would he return with friends?

A soft gasp behind him pulled his attention back to Patsy, who stood unsteadily, one hand braced against a boulder, her shoulders heaving.

"You all right?" He moved toward her.

She nodded. "I'm fine." Her gaze strayed to the place where the man had disappeared, something unreadable in the green depths. Vulnerability, perhaps. And fear.

Jonah swallowed hard, forcing himself to face the truth. "Do you realize who that was?" Maybe she hadn't gotten a good look at him in the fading light. It was hard to believe the man would come this far just to get his revenge. But he had, and he'd been thwarted. If anything, being run off like that would only make him angrier. What would stop him from trying again?

A shadow crossed her face, and she met his eyes. "Douglas. The man from the saloon." She straightened, gathering her composure around her like a cloak, her poker face sliding into place.

Shutting him out.

Disappointment twinged through him.

She was a tough woman, but she didn't have to carry every burden by herself.

She waded out of the creek, and he followed her. They could talk more back at camp.

But as he settled into making supper, Miss Whitman kept herself busy. She seemed to be trying to avoid talking about her attacker, and he couldn't bring himself to force the conversation.

The savory aroma of the stew wafted through the cool evening air as he ladled it into tin bowls. He handed one to Miss Whitman, and their fingers brushed for the briefest moment. The touch sent sparks through him.

But she gave no indication she'd felt anything, accepting the bowl with a murmured thank-you, her gaze distant and pensive.

They ate in silence, the crackle of the fire and the chirping of crickets the only sounds in the still night.

A few minutes later, Patsy set her bowl aside, drawing in a deep breath as if steeling herself. "Jonah, about the fight earlier..." She trailed off, her brow furrowing.

"Let me guess. You're going to tell me you had it under control?"

She shook her head, a rueful chuckle escaping. "Not this time. I...I don't know what would have happened if you hadn't stepped in. So thank you. Truly."

His tight jaw loosened as he studied her. She'd offered a real thank-you? He'd not expected that. "You're tougher than most, Patsy. I've no doubt you would've found a way to get free."

She poked at the fire with a stick. "Men like that—the ones who cheat and threaten—they're the kind you have to watch out for. They're evil, through and through." The bitterness in her voice spoke of painful experience.

Did he dare pry? "How long did you say you worked as a poker player?"

She sighed as her eyes took on a faraway look. "I came to Missoula Mills two months ago, after my husband died."

At the sorrow in her voice, an image of the graves back at the ranch slipped into his mind. Simple stones marked each one, pale in comparison to the grief of losing each person. First Dat, then Mum a week later. Then Lucy.

He pulled himself out of those thoughts before they swallowed him. She'd lost a husband. And recently. He wanted to ask more, to unravel the mystery of her past, but she'd built the walls protecting her heart for a reason, and he would not force his way through them.

Instead, he reached out, his hand hovering near hers for a moment before he thought better of it and pulled back. "I'm sorry for your loss."

She nodded, a sad smile playing at the corners of her mouth. "Thank you." Then she turned and began digging through her large satchel.

As he stared into the flames, his mind whirled with questions. How had her husband died? What had driven her to a life of gambling and danger? And why did Jonah find himself so desperate to know?

CHAPTER 5

*T*he noon summer sun shone high above as Patience rode beside Jonah along the winding trail that followed a creek through the woods. In the brightness of day with the pleasant murmur of water running over rocks, it was a little hard to remember the terror from the night before when Douglas attacked.

Yet he could be following them now. Jonah rode with his rifle across his lap, and she had her Derringer tucked in her sleeve where she could reach it with a twist of her wrist. But if Douglas had found another gun...

His rifle had been waterlogged last night, and he'd run off without it. So maybe they were safe. Maybe he'd decided to cut his losses and return to Missoula Mills.

Anyway, this journey was almost over. Jonah said they'd reach his family's ranch within the hour. The closer they traveled to his home, the lighter he seemed. The worry tensing his shoulders had eased, little by little, today.

He was a handsome man, with rugged features of one accustomed to working the land. His dark hair fell in waves under his wide-brimmed hat, and his features showed his strength. A set chin, steady blue eyes that seemed to see more than she liked sometimes. Those strong shoulders and the way he handled his horse with a confidence that many men didn't possess. She'd only known him a few long days, but the way he'd treated her so far made her want to trust him.

And she did *not* need to fall into that trap again.

This would be a good time to ask more about what had happened with her niece. And with her mother. And everything since. "Tell me," she said softly. "How did you find Anna? How long has it been?"

Jonah's blue eyes met hers, and a bit of pain shone there. Because he understood her need? Or because the story was such a hard one?

He faced forward again. "It was last winter. We saw smoke from a campfire at the cabin I was building. There wasn't a roof on it or anything, no shelter at all save the walls that might have blocked a bit of wind. When we went to check, there were signs someone had camped there, but they were gone."

His Adam's apple bobbed. "A hard snow storm came the next day. I don't know how they survived it." Again his throat worked. "If I'd known they were out in it..." He released a sigh. "A couple days later, Eric saw Anna running through the woods. Remember Eric? He's the one who married Naomi. Anyway, Anna was dressed like a boy. I went with Eric to follow her. She led us to their camp. Your mother..." This seemed hard for him. Was he reliving that day?

"Your mother was alive, but not conscious enough to talk to us. We got her and Anna back to the house as quick as we could. My sister-in-law—"

"Dinah, right? I think you told me she's a doctor?" Imagine that, a female physician. Of course, she was a female gambler. Her gender came in handy sometimes.

He nodded, one quick dip of his head. "Dinah did everything she could for her." He sent Patience a look thick with sorrow.

"She passed that evening. She didn't ever get to talk to us, so all we've had to go on was what Anna could tell us."

Patience's chest ached, her eyes blurring at the thought of what Mama had suffered those last days. Why had they traveled all this way? Jonah had said that they'd come to find her, but that couldn't be. Such a rough journey, and why hadn't Mama tried to contact her before setting out?

She ventured a safer version of the question. "You're sure Anna said they came to find me?"

"That's what she said, to visit her aunt Patsy who came here to get married."

Pain pressed in her chest. She'd forgotten that detail she'd added in the short letter she sent her mother. It felt wrong to go so far as the western territories without at least telling her mother about Michael's death. She'd not wanted Mama to worry that she'd be alone, so she'd included the part about her new husband-to-be. The man she was going west to marry.

Anger quickened her pulse. Jackson, that lying scoundrel.

Jonah was studying her, and by the look on his face, he seemed confused.

She forced her thought away from the man who'd lured her west and back to his story. "What happened next?"

"We knew we had to find you. Anna said her parents had both died, and it sounded like you were her only living relative." He shot her a look, his mouth crooked sideways. "We didn't have much to go on. Only the name Patsy and the fact that you have red hair."

For some reason, a grin found her own lips. "How long did it take you? Were your other brothers looking too?"

"At first, Eric helped. But then he and Naomi were to be married, and with all the wedding preparations..." He trailed off with a rueful chuckle. "I wasn't needed at the ranch, so it made sense for me to keep searching on my own." It seemed like he'd said all he was going to. But then he added in a quieter voice, "I guess I wanted some time away from the ranch myself."

There was something he wasn't saying, but since she didn't think it had anything to do with Anna, it wasn't her business to press. She didn't want him hounding her for more information about her past, so she'd best respect his privacy about his. Besides, they were riding up a steep slope now, so she should concentrate on her horse. And the trail.

The horses breathed heavily as they climbed.

A quarter hour later, a clearing shone through the trees ahead. Her heart picked up speed. Was this it? His home? His family?

Her niece?

They rode out of the woods and into the ranch yard. A barn and corrals stood in front of them, and a log house perched on a hill a little farther up, smoke curling from its stone chimney.

Jonah aimed toward the structure.

She followed, inhaling a steadying breath. This was it. She was about to see Anna for the first time in too many years. Would her niece be nervous to see her?

As they drew close, the cabin door swung open, and a lovely woman with honey-blond hair emerged, followed by a small girl clutching her skirts.

Patience's breath caught.

Anna.

Even from a distance, she recognized those wide, solemn eyes that reminded her so much of her sister. The girl had grown up in the five years they'd been apart. That long brown hair that matched both of her parents'.

Jonah reined in his horse and dismounted in one smooth motion.

Tears pricked Patsy's eyes as she slid off her horse. "Anna," she breathed, taking a step forward. Her arms ached to enfold her niece.

The woman, who must be Naomi, the one Jonah had said Anna was living with, smiled and gently nudged Anna forward. "Go on, sweetheart. It's your Aunt Patsy, come all this way to see you."

But Anna hung back, her small face uncertain as she gripped Naomi.

Patience's heart sank. Of course, it had been years. Anna had been just a toddling child when Patience left. She couldn't expect her to come running as if no time had passed.

Jonah crouched midway between Anna and Patience, his voice gentle. "Anna-bug, do you remember your Aunt Patsy? She's come a long way to see you."

Anna's eyes darted to Patience, then back to Jonah. Slowly, tentatively, she released her grip on Naomi's skirts and took a step forward. Then another.

Suddenly, she was in Patience's arms, her small body warm and solid against Patience's chest. Patience wrapped her arms around the thin form, tears threatening as she breathed in the sweet, childish scent of her. Her niece. Her family.

A sob broke free, and she stroked the girl's hair. "Oh, Anna, I've missed you so much. I'm sorry it's been so long."

She reveled in the feel of her, unsure how much time had passed when she finally lifted her head to meet Jonah's gaze. His green eyes shone with emotion, and she mouthed a silent thank-you.

Beyond him, Naomi dabbed at her cheeks, her smile tremulous.

But even as gratitude swelled in Patience's chest, a twinge of disappointment pricked at her heart. Anna had not run to her, had not even seemed to recognize her. There was so much lost time between them, so much trust to rebuild.

She didn't have time to mourn the thought, for a stream of other people reached them. Welcoming with eagerness and a multitude of questions. He waved down the cacophany and motioned to her, and the group quieted almost immediately, all eyes taking her in.

"Everyone, this is Miss Patsy Whitman." Jonah sent her a smile that eased the churning that had suddenly started in her middle. "Patsy, this is my family. My brother Jericho and his wife Dinah. Eric and Naomi, who you already met. Since their daughter Mary Ellen isn't here, I imagine she's napping. My niece Lillian, and Angela, my brother Jude's wife." He looked to Jericho. "I guess the rest of the boys are out with the animals?"

Jericho nodded, and Jonah turned back to her. "You'll meet Jude, Gil, Miles, and my nephew Sean tonight."

She brightened her smile for the group. "It's a pleasure to meet you all." And overwhelming.

The woman standing beside Jonah's brother stepped forward. Dinah was her name? She reached out to clasp Patsy's hand. "We're so glad you've come. We've been praying for this day."

A burning sensation pricked her eyes, but she ignored it. "Thank you. I'm so grateful Anna's been well-cared for." These people looked so much more...wholesome and good than she'd expected. Nothing like the line of hard-nosed brothers she'd imagined.

Eric spoke up. "She's a special little girl. We've come to love her as our own."

A flicker of unease slipped through her. They wouldn't try to stop her from taking Anna, would they? She was blood kin, after all. Anna's only living relative.

She glanced down at her niece. Anna gazed back up at her, curiosity and a hint of hope shining in those wide eyes so like her mother's.

Patsy drew in a fortifying breath. She was jumping at shadows. These people had been searching for her. Jonah had been searching for her. Since last year, he'd said.

Straightening her shoulders, Patsy met Jonah's steady gaze.

He seemed to understand the emotions swirling within her, offering a small nod of encouragement.

She turned back to the Coulters, summoning a grateful smile. "I can't thank you enough for all you've done. For taking in Anna when she had no one else. I know it couldn't have been easy, but I'm in your debt."

CHAPTER 6

*J*onah brushed a hand over the rough-hewn logs of his new cabin, the wood still fresh with the scent of pine. He and Patsy had only reached the ranch a few hours ago, and he'd come to inspect his cabin the first chance he could.

The rustle of footsteps in the grass sounded from the doorway, and he spun. His first instinct was to look for Patsy—maybe because she'd been lingering in his thoughts—but he'd left her settled at the main house with Anna and a few of the other women.

Jericho appeared in the open doorway, his wide shoulders filling the space as he paused to take in Jonah and the shell of the cabin Jonah had worked so hard on. Jericho always had such a commanding presence. Even a stranger would never doubt he was the elder brother, in charge on this ranch, even in a cabin that wasn't his.

Jonah glanced around the place, doing his best to see it through his brother's eyes. It almost looked like a home. He just needed to add the floor and chink the logs, and he'd be ready to move in. Well, he wouldn't have furniture yet, but it would only be him, so that didn't matter much. He'd rather bed down on wooden planks in his own home than keep sleeping in a bunkhouse like a hired hand.

Jericho glanced around, then ambled closer to Jonah. "Where's Sampson?"

Jonah cringed at the question. So much had happened with Patsy. That woman was enough to consume a fellow's waking thoughts with worries over her. But Sampson—and knowing he'd left him back in Missoula Mills—had never been far from Jonah's mind.

He turned to the corner and inspected a joint as though there were a flaw in it. "Had some things to do in Missoula. Said he'll come when he's ready. Probably a few more days."

Jonah didn't have to be looking to feel the weight of Jericho's disapproval hanging thick in the air. His oldest brother had come a long way from those days when he'd kept outsiders away from their ranch at gunpoint—and kept their family *in* with similar determination. But he'd put Jonah in charge of Sampson on their trip to take the necklace to convince Patsy. Jericho probably considered him leaving the lad behind as failing.

But Sampson was no longer a youth.

Jericho was the eldest of the boys in their family, but not the oldest child. Lucy had had that honor.

Swallowing the sting that still came with her memory, Jonah met Jericho's gaze and forced his voice to be strong and level. "Sampson's a grown man now. Nineteen. He knows the trail back. He said he would be along in a few days."

Jericho gave a single nod. Worry clouded his expression, but maybe he wouldn't voice it.

As the moment of quiet stretched, Jericho toed the ground with his boot. "So what're you gonna do with this woman? Anna's aunt?"

Not that it was his place to do anything with her, but Jonah couldn't deny that he'd been skirting around the topic in his own mind. They'd all wanted to find Anna's aunt and reunite the two. But what now? Did they want her to take Anna and be on her way?

Alone?

He couldn't help but remember the scoundrel who'd attacked her. What if Jonah hadn't been there to protect her? What if she'd been alone with Anna in the woods? What would have become of the two of them?

No, they couldn't just...just send them off.

Everything in him revolted at the thought.

He rubbed the back of his neck. "I don't rightly know. I found her and brought her back. I reckon I've done my part."

Jericho studied him, his gaze piercing in the fading daylight that filtered through the cabin door. "You sure about that? Seems to me there might be more to it, the way you look at her."

"I don't know what you're talking about," he snapped, but heat crept up his neck. He walked to the back wall, rubbing his fingers along a log's surface. Had Patsy thought he was ogling her? Had he been? No, of course not. Just... Well, he couldn't help but notice her. She wasn't exactly repulsive, after all. "She's Anna's kin, that's all. Not my concern beyond that."

"If you say so, little brother." Jericho's words held too much skepticism. "Just be careful. I doubt she's planning to hang around."

But perhaps, with the right motivation...

He had no idea what she planned. Would she take Anna back to Missoula Mills? Surely not. Anna would be better off staying with Naomi and Eric than spending days and nights hanging around a saloon.

Maybe Patsy would consider...

But he was a fool to even think it. She was a woman with her own mind. And he had a poor record when it came to convincing women to stay for him. He wasn't aching to go through that pain again.

Jonah turned toward the door. "We best be getting back. Supper will be on the table soon."

They trudged in silence to the main house. The aroma of roasted venison and freshly baked bread wafted out to greet them as they neared the cabin. Jonah's stomach rumbled.

Inside, Dinah, Angela, Naomi, and Lillian were setting the last dishes on the long trestle table. Patsy stood uncertainly to one side, her green eyes wide as she took in the flurry of activity. When she noticed Jonah, relief eased over her face.

Something inside him sprang to life at that expression. Maybe a little pleasure that she saw him as safe. Maybe a little sadness that she didn't feel comfortable around his family. Mostly though, a protectiveness that made him want to slip an arm around her and pull her close. Let her know that she didn't always have to show a brave front. She could rely on others— him—to help when she didn't feel comfortable.

He approached her, acutely aware of Jericho watching. "Everything all right?" he asked in a low voice.

She nodded, but the tension in her shoulders told him otherwise. "I'm just... I'm not used to all this," she whispered, her gaze darting around the room. "It's been a long time since I was part of a...family gathering." The way she said family put a bit of longing in the word.

Jonah's heart twisted at the wistfulness in her tone. He knew what it was like to feel like an outsider, even among one's own kin. Impulsively, he touched the small of her back. "You'll do just fine. We might as well take our seats."

He'd not known where to seat Patsy, but Dinah, smiling at their guest, pointed at the chair next to his usual spot. "Sit there. Anna will be beside you." It made sense that Patsy should sit beside her niece. And she should be next to him too. He knew her better than anyone else here, having traveled with her.

But did Dinah, like Jericho, think Jonah was attracted to her? Probably. They were married, and he could just picture the two gossiping about him.

The thought of his big brother brought a grin.

It didn't last, though. Did they really see that?

How could they have when he had no idea how he felt about this woman? Other than protective. Something about her made him want to show her she didn't have to always be so brave and capable and self-sufficient.

She could trust people sometimes. She could let her guard down now and again. She'd done that with him, during their trip up the mountain, and with Anna, when she'd hugged her niece.

But that protective wall was firmly back in place now. He watched his family bump up against it throughout the meal. Her polite expressions, the way she dodged and deflected questions. But somehow, she still trusted Jonah, watching him from the corner of her eye and taking her cues from his actions.

He tried to draw her into the conversation, hoping to set her at ease.

After the meal ended, he turned to her. "Do you want to go down to the barn and check on our horses? Make sure they're settled in all right for the night?" The horses were fine, of course. Miles would have seen to that. But Jonah needed to talk to Patsy alone, away from the curious gazes of his family.

Patsy's green eyes searched his face, maybe for his true reason for taking her outside. "That's a good idea."

When they stepped out into the cool evening air, the tension drained from his shoulders. Out here he could breathe easier. Think clearer.

As they walked, he studied her profile, the way the moonlight caught in her fiery hair. "Is everything all right? I know it's a lot to take in, being here with all of us."

She wrapped her arms around herself and sighed. "It's not

just that. It's Anna." She paused so long, it seemed she might not finish the thought. Then the last words slipped out. "I don't think she likes me very much."

* * *

*P*atience had admitted the truth. Something about this man nudged down her barriers and left her wanting to tell him things that made her too vulnerable. She'd vowed to never let a man have that kind of sway over her again.

Jonah stopped walking and faced her, his blue eyes full of concern. "What makes you say that? Did something happen?"

She shook her head, not wanting to go into details. "It's nothing specific. Just a feeling I get. Like she resents me being here, disrupting her life." Patience's chest tightened as she spoke the words aloud. Anna was the only family she had left. The thought that she might not want her was painful. She'd felt that way too often with her father.

"I'm sure that's not true." Jonah's voice was gentle. He squeezed her shoulder, the warmth of his touch seeping through her shirt. "This is all new for her too. Give her some time to adjust. She's been through a lot."

Patience blinked back the tears that threatened. He was right, of course. She couldn't expect Anna to welcome her without reservation, not when they barely knew each other. Not when Patience represented another upheaval in her life.

Jonah stared up into the cloudy night sky. "I remember how hard it was after my sister left, and I was nearly a grown man. I didn't know what to say to anyone. I tried to cover up how much I missed her."

Even now, a tinge of pain wove through his tone.

She couldn't help asking more. "I didn't realize you had a sister. What happened to her?"

"Lucy. She was the oldest." He shrugged as if it didn't matter, but it was clear in his expression she'd mattered a lot to him. "She met a man in Missoula Mills. A good-for-nothing miner who took her off to Virginia City. After the children were born, he got sick and died. Then she took ill a couple years ago."

His voice had lost all hint of emotion, stating mere facts. Lucy must have been important to him. What could Patience say to help, or at least show she understood? "It must have been hard to lose her."

Maybe he would think she meant at Lucy's passing, but it sounded like he'd really lost her when she'd chosen a miner over this brother who must have adored her.

Her throat ached with that too-familiar feeling.

As the youngest, Hannah had always been the chosen daughter in their family.

"She was special." His voice was strained as he looked at her. "She took the time to really see a person. To understand there's more than what you'd find on the surface. She always saw the good in people, even when it wasn't there."

A rueful smile tugged his lips. "When I was seven, I accidentally started a fire in our outhouse. I knocked over a lantern, and the whole thing just...poof... went up in flames. My brothers—even my pa—they ribbed me something fierce about it. But Lucy, she always stood up for me. Seemed to always see *me*, not just the things I did or the ways I messed up."

The image Patience's mind formed of that little seven-year-old made her want to reach out and pull him in. This man—so strong and capable—was still that boy, deep down. He needed someone to see through his tough exterior and understand the man inside.

She swallowed past the lump in her throat. "I'm glad you had her."

"Me too." He sighed. "What about you? Did you have someone like that?"

She shook her head, not gazing into the dark forest but at him. "If I had, I might not have landed in the mess I did."

More than she intended to admit. She crossed her arms over her chest. She had no desire to talk about her past and her poor choices.

Yet, as she dared meet his eyes, the way he was looking at her—probably the same way his sister had looked at him—made her want to tell her story. Maybe he wouldn't judge her for the things she'd done and the decisions she'd made. Maybe he'd understand why she'd done those things. Maybe he'd at least try.

She took a breath for courage. "My father always saw fault in me. It was...hard to grow up knowing everything I did would be berated or criticized. My sister could do no wrong. As soon as I could get away, I did.

"I was barely old enough to marry, but I met a man who swept me off my feet. A gambler. My family disapproved, of course, especially my father. No matter who I'd chosen—or who'd chosen me, Papa would've disapproved." Any man who wanted Patience must be flawed. But she didn't say that aloud. "He told me I could never make a marriage with Michael work."

Jonah's expression so warm and earnest, giving her the strength to go on.

"Of course, Papa's lack of faith in us—in me—only made me more determined to prove him wrong. I married Michael, much to my family's dismay, and at first, things were wonderful. He was charming and attentive, treating me like I was the only woman in the world. We lived on riverboats, where gambling was good every single night. I learned his tricks. He taught me to shoot...really well." Those had been good days, back when she'd still believed in marriage. In them. "I thought if I could just be a part of his world, support him in what he did, it would be enough to make our marriage strong."

She breathed out the tension in her chest. "It didn't. The gambling led to his downfall in the end. He was playing a game one night when another man accused him of cheating. The man...he shot Michael right there. Then he turned on me, said I'd better pay up all the money Michael had supposedly stolen from him the night before."

A shudder slid down her spine at the memory. The glint of the gun in the lamplight. The acrid scent of gunpowder and blood. The rage and accusation in the man's eyes.

"If not for the barkeep, who tackled the killer, I'd be dead. I ran. Thank God, we were at port. But I'd been around that life long enough to know that the guy, even if there were a lawman around to arrest him, would probably be released within a couple of hours." Her throat ached, but she forced out the words. " I found a place to hide, then took the first opportunity to head west, to get as far from that murderer as possible. Just in case he was serious about making me pay that debt."

Jonah studied her. "Why west? Why didn't you go home?"

She raised her brows. "And prove my father right?" But she sighed. "Honestly, I probably would've, except I was afraid he'd find me. I figured he'd be less likely to follow me into the wilds of Montana than back to Boston."

Jonah took her hand, his calloused fingers warm and strong around hers. "Is that why you were so suspicious of me when we first met?"

She nodded, blinking back the tears that had welled up. "I thought you might be working for him. I'm sorry I doubted you."

He squeezed her hand. "No reason to apologize. You were protecting yourself the only way you knew how. I understand that."

She searched his face, seeing the truth of his words etched there. He did understand. More, she thought, than anyone else ever had. He knew what it was to be judged for the surface of things, for the mistakes and missteps. He knew what it was to need someone to look deeper, to see the true heart beneath.

Just as Lucy had done for him, he now did for her. Offering her the gift of being seen. Of being known.

It was almost too much to take in. She had to look away, deep into the woods, drawing in a shaky breath.

"You know you're safe here, Patsy. Right? We won't let anyone hurt you, no matter who comes."

Safe. The word felt foreign, unfamiliar. When was the last time she had truly felt safe? She couldn't remember.

But as she turned to meet his gaze, the determination there wrapped around her like a warm blanket. Maybe, just maybe... he was right.

CHAPTER 7

The afternoon sun filtered through the cabin windows as Patience sat in a chair by the fire cutting apples for after-dinner pies. Beside her, Anna was still and silent in a small armchair, her small hands clasped tightly in her lap. In one of the bed chambers, Naomi was putting her one-year-old daughter, Mary Ellen, down for a nap. This wasn't her home, she'd brought Anna and the little one over that morning so Patience could have plenty of time with Anna. This was her first full day at the ranch, and she wanted every moment she could with her niece.

Anna didn't seem to approve of the plan.

Patience'd had to practically force the girl to sit with her, and now she didn't seem inclined to talk at all. She hadn't realized a seven-year-old could be so sullen.

"That's a pretty dress you're wearing." Patience nodded toward the pink floral print of the gown that fit her niece perfectly.

"Naomi made it." Anna sent a sideways glare at her, as though Patience had refused to provide clothing.

She forced a smile. "She's a talented seamstress." Maybe if

she acknowledged how wonderful Eric and Naomi—and all these people—had been to Anna, it would help break down the barrier. "I'm so glad Naomi and the others here have been so kind."

Anna shrugged, but Patience didn't miss the tremble of her lower lip. *Oh, Anna.* Patience's heart ached at all the pain this sweet girl had endured. All the loss.

She reached across the chasm between them and rubbed her thin shoulders. "I'm so glad you've had them. I know it was so hard when grandmother got sick." Was that what the girl thought had happened to her? From what Patience could gather, they didn't know for sure whether Mama had been ill or succumbed to the elements. Maybe it was a combination of the two.

Anna sniffed, fighting, it seemed, to keep from showing all her emotions. Patience kept rubbing her shoulders. "You know, your grandmother was my mother. I miss her." The sting of tears burned her throat, cracking her voice. She'd better find a better topic soon or they'd both be a soggy mess. She fingered the necklace she hadn't taken off since Jonah gave it to her. "These beads remind me of her."

Anna sent her a sideways glance, once again almost glaring. Hadn't Jonah said Anna treasured the necklace? Maybe she felt Patience had stolen it from her, taken the one thing she had to remember her grandmother by.

Patience unfastened the clasp. At least this she could remedy. And she could share the story behind the heirloom. "This first belonged to my grandmother—your great-grandmother."

As Patience placed the beads in Anna's small hands, the girl studied them.

Patience leaned in a little, stroking Anna's shoulders with her fingers once more. "Would you like to hear the story of how she was given them?"

Anna's head lifted slightly, curiosity flicking in her eyes.

"Before she met Grandpa Ben, Grandma was a nurse, and she traveled all over the world helping people. One time, she even went to South America to the Amazon rainforest and lived with the natives there for several months."

Anna's eyes widened, though she might not know what the Amazon was. Patience described it as best she could from what Grandma Annie had told her—the lush green jungle, the exotic animals, the kind and generous people who had welcomed her grandmother into their midst. "And when it was time for her to leave, the natives gave her this necklace as a gift, to thank her for all she had done. She treasured it always and passed it down to my mother. Grandma was so brave and loved adventure. She used her talents to help others. And do you know what?"

Patience waited and was soon rewarded with a quiet, "What?"

"Your mama named you after her. Her name was Anna Marie Masters, but I always called her Grandma Annie."

Anna's eyes shone, and for the first time since Patience arrived, she seemed truly happy in Patience's presence. A wave of love swept through her, so full it filled every part of her. *Thank You, God, for giving me another chance with this sweet girl.*

* * *

*P*atience studied the faces around the table, especially Jonah's youngest brother, Miles, who was riffling through the crate of games. They'd finished dinner, and Dinah and Naomi were slicing apple pie for dessert, but the steady patter of rain on the roof had made the group restless.

Miles straightened, a deck of cards in his hand. "I say we play poker."

Her middle tightened. Poker? Surely there was something else they could choose that wouldn't make her feel...dirty.

"Not poker." Jonah's voice rumbled strong at her side.

Thank you.

Miles looked up from the crate, his brows furrowed. "Why not poker? It's not like we're betting real money. I'm tired of chess, so it has to be some kind of cards."

Patience forced herself not to shift in her seat as unease settled in her stomach like a cold stone. She'd spent too many nights in smoky saloons, the clink of coins and the shuffle of cards the melody of her shame. This place felt so...different. So untainted. The last thing she wanted to do was mar the memories she was making here.

"Let's play Rounds." Gil nudged a pack of cards in Miles's hand.

Miles shrugged, pulling out the worn deck. "Rounds it is, then."

Soon, Dinah and Naomi brought plates full of sweet apple pie, and the cards had been dealt. A surprising number of the family had opted to watch rather than participate. If she'd known that was a choice, she would have done the same. But she'd been one of the first asked to play, so she'd committed. In the end, the players had been Miles, Gil, their niece, Lillian, and herself. From what she'd pieced together, Lillian and her brother, Sean, were Lucy's children, who'd come to the ranch after their mother passed from the illness Jonah had spoken of.

The sweet aroma of pie and the camaraderie around the table made the game nothing like an evening in the saloon. She might have even been able to play poker without it feeling like she'd gone back to that other place. These Coulters were unlike any family she'd ever seen.

Boisterous and joking, yet kind and considerate. They weren't afraid to confront when someone stepped out of line, yet there was always an undertone of love, as if nothing the other person did or said could ever stop them from being part of the family.

So very different from the family she'd been raised in. They made it hard to think of the people she'd grown up with—especially her father—as family at all. Not when she applied the same term to these Coulters.

Their first game became the best two out of three, then the best three out of five as Gil's competitive streak grew with each lost hand.

Patience did her best not to win every hand, but all three of her opponents were so easy to read, she couldn't seem to stop herself from responding to their cues.

Still, she did manage to lose one game to Miles, and she kept her margin of winning small on the others. More than that, she had fun. The banter between the brothers, both those playing and those watching as they licked pie from their forks, made her smile. Even Lillian joined in, showing her quick wit and charm.

It wasn't until Patience glanced at Jonah after their fourth game that she realized he wasn't smiling. Did it bother him that she'd won so much? Maybe he thought she should have allowed Lillian the chance. She should have, and Gil too. The others wanted to play another hand, but she declined as politely as she could.

Jonah was the first to stand, his chair scraping against the wooden floor. "I'll go get a load of firewood before I head to the bunkhouse."

Her heart leapt at the chance to talk with him alone. She could find out what she'd done wrong so she didn't make the mistake again. He was forthright enough to tell her without being mean. She followed him out into the misty night where the damp air clung to her skin.

She caught up to him at the corner of the house, his broad shoulders hunched against the wet chill.

"Jonah, wait." Her voice sounded small in the vastness of the night.

He turned to her, his expression unreadable in the cloudy night.

She paused in front of him. "What's wrong?"

His eyes met hers, a hint of wariness in their depths. "Nothing's wrong, Patience. Just tired is all."

"Was it the card game? Did I do something to offend you or the others by winning too much?"

He gave a humorless chuckle. "Nothin' like that. Everyone had a grand time." Yet bitterness tinged his voice.

"Then what is it? If I made some mistake, I want to know so I don't repeat it."

He sighed, rubbing a hand over his face. "I didn't realize how talented you were at cards. If I didn't know better, I'd say you were cheating." He paused, shaking his head. "Though I can't think of a way to cheat at Rounds."

Patience wasn't sure if his words were meant as a compliment or an insult. "I just watch for tells. People always show what kind of hand they have, if you're watching closely enough."

His eyebrows raised. " Like what?"

She wasn't one to share her secrets, but there couldn't be harm in telling him what she'd observed. "Well, Miles's left eyebrow twitches when he has a good pair. Lillian taps her fingers on the table when she's close to going out. And Gil..." She couldn't help but chuckle. "The more he tries to conceal his hand, the easier it is to know what he's thinking."

By the time she finished, Jonah wore an expression somewhere between a smile and a smirk. "So, what's my tell then?"

The question caught her short. His? But even as she thought the word, she immediately knew her answer. In fact, he was doing it now. She met that intense gaze. "Your eyes. They twitch at the outside corners, just a little, when you're deciding whether you want to be serious or not."

He pulled back. "They do not." His words were firm, but

there was a playful light in his eyes—and that unmistakable twitch.

She lifted her brows, reaching up to touch the spot, just so he'd know where she meant.

But the moment her fingers brushed his skin, heat from the contact nearly seared the pads of her fingers. Awareness sparked between them, and there was no amusement in his gaze now.

He was so close. Close enough that he could move in a little and take her lips with his.

He didn't look away. She felt frozen even before he captured her wrist in his warm hand. Even in his gentle grip, she could feel his power, though he was incredibly gentle as he lowered her hand. But instead of releasing her, he slid his fingers until their hands were palm to palm. Then he slid his hand around hers so it cradled the back of her hand, palm up. His thumb stroked her palm in a movement that stole her breath, his eyes intense as they locked with hers.

"Patsy..." His low voice sent a shiver through her that had nothing to do with the damp chill. "You matter to me." His eyes dipped to her mouth, and she could feel the intensity of his gaze in her belly before it lifted to meet hers again. "I'd really like to kiss you right now."

A thrill sizzled through her, but she had to stop this, to pull back. She had to protect her heart from this man who threatened to topple all her carefully constructed walls. She couldn't let herself get too close, not when she had plans to leave, to finally pursue her dreams. That peaceful cottage in the valley. Freedom from the control of any man. Even this one, as tempting as he was right now. He wouldn't always be like this. No man could be trusted.

He seemed to sense her inner turmoil. His thumb stilled, but his grip on her hand tightened, anchoring her in place.

"But I won't." His gaze never wavered in hers. "Because you

matter to me, and I don't ever want you to feel like you're not safe with me. Not for any reason."

The weight in her chest eased. She'd never had a man put her feelings or her comfort above his own desires.

Jonah made her feel cherished and respected. If only it would last.

With a tenderness that made her heart ache, he lifted her hand and pressed a lingering kiss to her palm. The contact sent a tingle racing up her arm, spreading through her body like wildfire. Then he released her and walked to the stack of firewood, where he gathered an armload.

In that moment, a part of her wished he hadn't been so noble, that he'd thrown aside his caution and kissed her like she knew he wanted to. Like she wanted him to, despite her fears.

But as Jonah straightened, the logs cradled against his chest, reality crashed around her. She couldn't afford to get lost in foolish fantasies, not when she had Anna to think about. She had plans, dreams that were finally within reach. Dreams that didn't include getting tangled up with a rancher, no matter how kind and handsome he might be at first.

He would change. Right? She'd seen no sign of it yet, but surely she would.

CHAPTER 8

*S*omething tugged Patience from sleep, and she squinted in the dim light of her room. Had she overslept? Sunlight shone through the window curtains.

A muffled shout sounded from the main room. As she pushed herself up on one elbow, the words became clearer.

"—should've sent me instead! I would've made sure it got done right." That was Miles' voice, loud and angry. She'd never heard him like that before. It shouldn't surprise her though. He was a man, after all.

"You think you're the only one who can handle stock?" Jericho's tone matched his brother's. "I could've done it if you'd let me."

Gilead said something too low for her to make out.

Patience slipped out of bed and padded to the door, cracking it open to peer into the main room. The three brothers stood in a tense triangle, faces flushed and eyes flashing.

"I'm the oldest. It's my responsibility to take care of things." Jericho spoke through gritted teeth.

"And look how well that turned out," Miles shot back. "Half the herd scattered to God knows where."

"It wasn't half the herd," Jericho growled.

The front door opened, and all three men turned to see who would enter. Jonah stepped inside.

Miles waved a hand at him. "And that's another problem around here."

Jonah's head jerked back, his eyes widening.

Miles pushed on. "How could you leave our brother in Missoula Mills? You were in such an all-fired hurry to get back here, as if that redhead couldn't have waited a couple more days. But you just got all swoony-eyed over her and didn't care a wit about Samson. For all we know, he might be dead now. Killed in a barroom fight or who knows what else."

Jonah's wide eyes had narrowed, and he stood by the closed door, his hands braced at his hips. When Miles finished, Jonah strode forward, his long legs bringing him up close to his youngest brother. "You'd better keep a civil tongue, boy. If you ever speak of Patsy as anything other than Miss Whitman, I'll take you out back and teach you some manners with Dat's belt just like I used to. And Sampson's fine. He's got more sense than you, that's sure an' certain."

Patience eased out a breath. Jonah had stood up for her. She might not like the raised voices, but at least his had been raised in her defense. That didn't usually happen.

Gilead moved toward them. "Settle down, all o' ya. We've got strays to find."

Jericho raked a hand through his hair, exhaling heavily. His gaze flicked to the side and locked with Patience's through the crack in the door. A flash of annoyance touched his eyes before he turned away. "I'll head out now, see if I can't round up them strays afore they wander too far off." He reached for his hat.

"I'll come with you," Gilead said.

"No." Jericho's reply brooked no argument. "You go with Miles and Sean to work the two-year-olds. Jude needs Jonah today. I'll manage on my own." He strode out, letting the door bang shut behind him.

Miles kicked at a chair leg, muttering under his breath. Gilead just sighed, suddenly looking much older than his young years. He was younger than Patience, she was almost sure of it.

As the men turned and left the cabin, she eased her door closed. By the time she'd dressed and pinned up her hair, the knot in her middle had almost eased. That argument felt too much like how her father used to speak to people—her especially. Always berating.

Then with Michael. He wasn't always cross, mostly just when he'd started drinking for the day. Drinking and gambling went together, so there was rarely a day he didn't imbibe.

She let out a sigh and stepped from her chamber into the main room. Dinah and Lillian worked near the cookstove.

Patience approached them, schooling her features into a pleasant expression. "Good morning. Is there anything I can do to help?"

Dinah glanced over at her, a bright smile lighting her face. As though there hadn't just been a tense argument right here in her house. "Good morning. Did you sleep well?"

Patience dipped her chin. "I did. How can I help you here?"

Dinah turned to pour batter into a frying pan. "Would you set plates and forks on the table? These johnny cakes will be ready soon."

"Of course." Patience moved to the shelf where the plates were kept. As she pulled them down, she searched for a way to broach her question. "I couldn't help overhearing the disagreement earlier. Is everything all right? The men sounded upset."

Dinah sighed, her shoulders slumping slightly as she stirred a pot of oats over the fire. "Jericho heard a wildcat last night, so he went out to check the cattle this morning. I guess the herd got spooked and scattered. The boys are worried about them is all. And about Sampson too. Tempers can flare when folks are afraid for the people they love."

Love. The word echoed in her mind. The Coulter family seemed to truly care for one another, but love was not a concept she associated with men. At least not the men in her life. Her father's *love*—if one could call it that—had been as hard and unyielding as his fists. And Michael...well, she'd mistaken his flattery and attention for love, only to discover too late the depths of his selfishness.

But Jonah had defended her honor just now. Stood up to his own brother for speaking ill of her. Perhaps there were different kinds of love in this world. Ones she had yet to understand.

"Lillian, would you get another bucket of water for us? We'll need a second pot of coffee." Dinah's smooth voice had a calming effect that seemed to settle the tension that lingered in the room.

Lillian headed toward the door, pail in hand. As she stepped outside, the sound of a male voice drifted through the open door.

"Careful with that bucket, girl! I just had to make new handles for two of 'em, and now I know why they keep breaking." Miles' tone was sharp and critical.

Patience sucked in a breath and set the remaining plates on the table. He was the youngest of the Coulter brothers, but he'd likely witnessed this kind of berating behavior from the older men and thought it acceptable. Well, she would show him otherwise.

She strode purposefully to the door. She would give Miles a piece of her mind, even if she was a visitor here. But as she stepped out into the bright morning sunlight, she paused. Lillian stood straight and tall, the bucket hanging easily from her small hand as she stared Miles down with a defiant tilt to her chin.

"I know how to carry a bucket, Uncle Miles." Her voice was

calm but firm. "Mama taught me well. I'll thank you not to speak to me that way."

Miles blinked, taken aback by the young girl's self-assured response. He opened his mouth as if to retort, then seemed to think better of it. With a dismissive shake of his head, he turned on his heel and stalked toward the barn.

Pride swelled in Patience's chest as she watched Lillian march to the side of the house where the water wagon was parked, her blonde braid swinging with each determined step. The girl had a strength in her, a quiet resilience that Patience recognized all too well. It was the same fortitude that had seen her through countless hardships in her own life.

Lillian would need it, for men were all the same. Maybe Jonah was different, but she couldn't stay here much longer and let Anna be subjected to the rest of the men here who couldn't control their tempers.

* * *

*J*onah paused in the kitchen doorway, a load of firewood filling one arm as he took in the sight before him.

Patsy and Lillian stood side by side at the cookstove, their heads bent together in concentration as Lillian showed Patsy how to adjust the damper. Golden light from the oil lamp cast a warm glow over their faces, making Patsy's red hair shimmer enough to catch his breath. The sweet smell of cinnamon and sugar filled the air, which seemed just the right scent to surround Patsy. She sure was a pretty thing, with those rich green eyes.

He moved closer, and both ladies looked up. Patsy's expression softened into a soft smile that looked like it was meant just for him. Maybe he was fooling himself, but every part of him came to life when she was near.

Maybe he should've kissed her the other night by the wood-shed. But that startled look in her eyes had clinched something inside him. Part of her might have wanted his kiss, but there was a piece in her that still hadn't learned to trust him. So many men had let her down through the years, abusing her innocent trust, turning on her when she needed them most. He wouldn't do the same to her, not for anything in the world.

He closed the distance to the kitchen area, and the women stepped away from the cookstove to give him access.

He added more wood to the firebox, causing a log inside to shift. Sparks tumbled out like a waterfall, and he jumped back as they scattered across the floor. He stomped on them, but a couple weren't so easy extinguished

He'd seen how fast a fire could catch, and he wasn't taking any chances.

A water bucket sat nearby, a cloth draped over the top. He jerked the fabric off so he douse the sparks with water.

As he lifted the cloth, bright flames flared to life, hungrily licking at the fabric. One of the sparks must've popped up.

A scream sounded behind him.

No reason to panic. He had it under control. He dropped the cloth and stomped out the fire, but another spark had lit the braided rug.

He was about to dump the water onto it when he glanced inside, just to be sure.

Not water but grease!

He jerked it back, whirling to get it away from the flames before it exploded like blasting powder.

Jericho rushed past him into the kitchen, muttering under his breath as he stomped out the remaining flames.

Jonah didn't stop until he'd carried the bucket out of the cabin and several more steps away. He set it down in the grass, pausing to catch his breath. His heart hammered as the adrenaline faded.

That had been a close call. If that grease had caught fire...

Footsteps sounded behind him, and he turned to see Jericho striding out of the cabin. "Trying to burn the place down again, little brother?" He was teasing, but his words soured in Jonah's stomach. "This sturdy house wouldn't have burned as fast as that outhouse did."

Did he really have to bring that up? Every time a spark blew the wrong direction, Jericho reminded him of that childhood offense. He'd been seven, for crying out loud.

Behind Jericho, Patsy was framed in the doorway, concern etched on her face.

Shame heated his neck. He lowered his gaze and moved around his brother. Best get in and see what the damage was. Hopefully nothing worse than a layer of black to scrub off the floor.

As he stepped into the house, Patsy moved outside, her skirts swishing past him. Where was she headed?

He turned just inside the doorway to see what she was doing. She looked like a woman with something on her mind.

She planted herself in front of Jericho with her hands on her hips. "And just why would you say a thing like that? Accidents happen. Jonah put out the fire before Lillian or I knew what was happening, and he wasn't the one who left a bucket of grease right next to the stove. Seems to me he handled it just fine."

Jonah stared at Patsy's rigid back, warmth flooding his chest. Here she was, standing up to his brother on his behalf. Defending him.

He couldn't recall the last time someone had done that.

Lillian stood beside him, taking in the stand-off in the yard.

"Uh…" Jericho didn't seem to know how to answer her. He ran a hand behind his neck. "I didn't mean to offend, ma'am."

Wow. She'd gotten to him if he was calling her ma'am.

"It's just a joke. Something we've always ribbed him about."

"Well." The sharp line of Patsy's shoulders eased, and when

she spoke, her voice gentled. "It seems like scratching at a sore again and again for years would make it hard to heal."

A sudden burn clogged Jonah's throat, especially when Jericho turned caught him standing there. He had to fight to keep from edging back into the shadows. She was right, though. That wound hadn't ever healed, not really.

Maybe if he'd stood up for himself way back when like she was standing up for him now, he wouldn't still be carrying that sting of shame.

But even as a boy, he'd never been one for confrontation. He'd always figured it was better to just let things go, not make waves. Keep the peace.

Looking at Patience, Jericho cleared his throat. "I suppose you have a point." He turned to Jonah once more, stepping to the base of the stoop. "I'm sorry. I know you didn't mean to burn down the outhouse. And I know you didn't mean to let those sparks out just now. I shouldn't have heckled you about it, not ever." He swallowed. "Will you forgive me?"

Those were hard words to say, but Jericho spoke with an earnestness that left no doubt he meant them.

Jonah nodded. "Of course." Though he knew well saying he'd forgive and doing it were two different things.

Jericho turned to Patsy then, and made a motion like he was pretending to doff his hat, though he wasn't wearing one. "Thank you, ma'am, for calling me out." He met Patsy's gaze squarely. "I love my brothers. My whole family. The last thing I'd want to do is hurt them. I appreciate you seeing what I didn't and righting the wrong."

Beside Jonah, Lillian let out a sigh. "My word, that woman can work miracles."

He'd missed Patsy's response to Jericho, but it appeared to have been trivial. He sent his niece a smile. "You're right there." Though he'd been part of the interchange just now, he still wasn't certain it had really happened. Patsy had stood up for him, and his brother had actually apologized.

Lillian sent him a knowing smile. "Aren't you glad now that you didn't marry Naomi?"

Jonah's breath caught, and he nearly reached out to clamp a hand over the girl's mouth. She'd already spoken the words though—loudly.

Her eyes rounded as she realized she'd said something that might not be common knowledge.

It took all his courage to turn and see if Patsy had heard.

She stood on the stoop, her gaze shifting from Lillian to him. Should he explain?

He'd not told her about Naomi, about how close he'd come to marrying her, how the cabin he was nearly finished building had been intended to house her and Mary Ellen after the wedding. But when Eric had shown up, Mary Ellen's father and her true love, she'd chosen Eric, a decision Jonah had known was right even at the time.

That knowledge hadn't lessened the sting of rejection. He'd been set aside the moment someone better came along.

Now, if there was to be anything between himself and Patsy, any chance of something real and true, he needed to tell her everything.

But what if she judged him for nearly marrying a woman he didn't love? Or what if she started to look for all the reasons Naomi had changed her mind before their wedding day? The thought made his stomach twist. His errors were plenty, and Patsy would find them easily enough. He was impulsive, stubborn, occasionally moody. His family judged him as less dependable than his brothers, no matter how hard he worked on the ranch and in the mine. He still even had a bit of a limp from when that wagon had run over him two years back.

Yep, Patsy was sure to find all the reasons he didn't measure up.

Even so, he had to tell her the truth, give her the chance to reject him now before he let himself get too attached.

"Well," Lillian said in what had probably been too long a silence. "Best get the floor swept, then we need to finish those cinnamon crisps. We'll have a bunch of hungry people for dinner soon, so we don't have much time left."

She motioned for Patsy to follow her back to the cooking area of the main room. Patsy gave him a quick glance as she passed by.

He didn't miss the questions in her eyes.

Maybe he could pull her aside tonight so they could talk. It was time he was honest with her. About everything.

CHAPTER 9

*P*atience's boots crunched in the dry grass as she made her way through the warm sunshine toward Jonah's new cabin, a basket of food tucked under her arm. She couldn't get Lillian's story out of her mind—how noble and self-less Jonah had been to offer marriage to Naomi, to provide a home for her and little Mary Ellen. The thought made Patience's heart flutter in a way that was becoming all too familiar when it came to the brooding, kindhearted cowboy.

Then when Eric had shown up, he and Naomi had reconciled, and Jonah had gallantly stepped back and let the three form the family they were clearly meant to be. The fact that Eric had searched so hard for Naomi was remarkable in itself.

As Patience neared the cabin, doubts crept in, casting shadows over her hopeful mood. Jonah had acted strangely last night and this morning. Was he avoiding her because he still carried a torch for Naomi? The idea sent a pang through her chest. She couldn't blame him if he did—Naomi was lovely inside and out.

Then there was the matter of that tender moment Patience and he had shared last week. Heat rose in her cheeks at the memory of Jonah's intense gaze, his gentle touch on her hand as he'd confessed his desire to kiss her.

But she valued Jonah's friendship too much to let a little embarrassment sour the openness between them. She'd never had a friend she could trust so completely to be on her side. Jonah was the real thing. A man of integrity. She'd seen enough of the *other* kind to know this when she spotted it. And his actions toward Naomi only confirmed that fact.

She would simply explain to him that Lillian had told her the whole story, and that her respect for him had only grown. She wouldn't hold him to his words said in a heated moment. Their friendship was too precious to let anything mar it.

Resolve strengthened, Patience approached the cabin. He wasn't working out front, and there was no door mounted yet, so she peered into the dark interior. Empty. She called out loudly enough for him to hear if he was behind the structure. "Jonah?"

"In the back." His voice was muffled, clearly coming through at least one solid wall.

She stepped back outside and turned to go around the left side. When she rounded the rear corner, Jonah was there, sleeves rolled up, brown curls tumbling over his brow as he worked. At the sight of her, he set his bucket on the ground and brushed his hands together, an unreadable expression flitting across his face.

"I brought you some lunch." Patience kept her voice bright as she held up the basket. "Thought you might be hungry after all this work."

He wiped a forearm across his brow, leaving a dark gray mark where the sweat had been. "That's kind of you, but I brought some food with me this morning."

She tilted her head and bit back a smile. She'd seen what he stuffed into his pockets. "A biscuit and an apple hardly count as a proper meal for a grown man putting in a hard day's work. I have sliced ham, fresh bread baked this morning with straw-berry jam, and those cinnamon crisps you seemed to enjoy so much last night."

Jonah's eyes lit as she lifted the napkin, revealing the tempting spread. "Well, I guess I could do with a bit of fortifica-tion. Thank you." He took the basket but didn't pull anything out, just stood there, like he was waiting for her to leave.

She motioned to a log lying nearby. "Sit and dig in."

He obeyed, and she settled in beside him, the rough bark pressing through her skirts. How to start? He'd lifted aside the cloth covering and was staring at the food as though his mind were elsewhere. She needed to get this out so they could both have peace.

She cleared her throat. "I wanted to...well, I wanted to talk to you about something."

Jonah looked at her, a guardedness in his posture and a tightness around his eyes that made her nerves jangle.

She clasped her hands in her lap, her fingers twining together. "Lillian told me the story last night. About you and Naomi. And what you offered to do for her and little Mary Ellen."

Jonah swallowed hard, his expression shuttering. "Did she now."

"I just wanted you to know that your actions, they were the mark of a truly honorable man. It took a strength of character, a selflessness, to make such an offer. And then, when Eric returned, to step back and let them be a family." She shook her head, at a loss for words to describe the admiration welling inside her.

Jonah was silent, his gaze fixed forward, forest blocking the horizon.

She soldiered on, the words tumbling out in a rush. "What I'm trying to say is, I understand if your heart still rests with Naomi. And I don't want you to feel beholden to...to anything that might have passed between us. Your friendship is important to me, and I'll be moving on soon anyway."

The silence stretched tight. Then Jonah turned to face her, his blue eyes intense. "It doesn't bother you that Naomi rejected me?"

She gaped at him. "Are you joking? I can't believe she let you go. What woman wouldn't leap at the chance to..." She broke off, heat flooding her cheeks at what she'd nearly said.

Jonah was still staring at her, an unreadable expression on his face. Slowly, deliberately, he set aside the basket. "Patsy..."

The way he said her name—the nickname she'd always hated. The one she'd determined never to allow when she came west—made heat sweep through her. She'd be happy to hear him say it anytime.

His eyes locked on hers with an intensity that made her chest tighten. "Your friendship is important to me too. *You* are important to me."

When his gaze dropped to her lips, she couldn't breathe. The air between thickened with a delicious tension. She couldn't look away from those piercing blue eyes, the determination in them sending a shiver down her spine.

When he leaned in, everything around her blurred. Her head went light, maybe because she'd stopped breathing. And when his warm, callused fingers cupped her jaw, her eyelids fluttered closed. That was why she had no warning before his lips brushed hers, sending a jolt through her that made her lean closer and pour herself into his kiss.

And oh, what a kiss.

She melted into him. Her hands curling in the fabric of his shirt, she anchored herself against the tide of sensation.

His tongue traced the seam of her lips, and she parted for him on a sigh, letting him taste her as she'd longed for him to do.

He explored her mouth with exquisite thoroughness, stoking

the embers of desire into flames that licked along her nerve endings. When he pulled back—too soon—the haze he'd brought over her made it impossible to speak more than his name. "Jonah." How could she put words to the riot of emotions swirling inside her?

He brushed his thumb along her cheekbone, the touch unbearably gentle. When he spoke, his voice was low and rough with emotion. "Patsy, I'm not pining for Naomi. It's you I want. Your friendship, yes. But more than that." His tenor dipped lower. "I want a chance to court you properly. To show you the kind of man I can be."

Tears pricked at the backs of her eyes. No one had ever wanted to court her, to cherish her, to prove himself worthy of her. All her life, she'd fought and scraped for survival, building walls around her heart. Yet with a few earnest words, Jonah had her defenses crumbling.

But she couldn't lose her focus.

She'd wanted to clear the air with Jonah, but she still had to leave. She had plans, a lifelong dream that was finally within reach. She would be independent, her and Anna, and not have to worry about how she would feed or protect herself. Nor would she be under the control of another man. They'd have their own little cottage, just like in the painting. And she wouldn't have to rely on anyone.

She straightened, pulling back to put space between them. How to say this without wrecking this friendship she truly wanted to protect? It might not withstand the blow she was about to give it.

"Jonah." She worked for a smile. "You're such an admirable man. I'm honored beyond words that you would ask." That sounded trite, so insignificant in the face of that kiss they'd just shared.

She swallowed the burn that crept to her eyes. "I can't stay here though. I have plans. I…" What a slap in the face to tell him her dream was more important than he was. But was there any other way to say it? She needed to be clear about her answer, lest he hold onto false hope. "I've had this dream for as long as I remember. To buy property in Indiana. There's a certain place. And a house."

He'd already slipped that shutter back over his eyes, and his arms had lowered to rest on his thighs. He picked at a blade of grass, and the way he didn't meet her gaze made her chest ache.

"If I didn't have this all worked out, Jonah, I would say yes. In a heartbeat." Would he question why she wasn't asking him to think about coming along? She had no good answer to that question. Only that this was something she had to do herself. Besides, his family was here. He'd built a cabin here with his own two hands. His entire life was here.

It would be unfair of her to pull him away.

He lifted his focus from the grass in his hands to stare ahead, toward the cabin wall. "I understand." She couldn't tell by the tone of his voice whether he really did or not.

She touched his arm to help him feel the weight of her next words. Beneath the fabric of his shirt, his muscle went stiff. Like a tree trunk. The man was more solid than the logs he'd felled for this house.

She forced her mind back on what she'd been about to say. "I'm sorry, Jonah. And I really meant what I said before. Your friendship is important to me. More so than..." Her voice quivered, and she paused.

He turned to her then, his mouth curving into a smile that almost met his eyes. "It's all right, Patsy. Our friendship is safe. I'm here for you. Anytime."

His words struck her with a new thought. *He* was here for *her*.

Was this friendship as one-sided as that sounded? Did she ever do things to help him, simply for his good, with no other motive?

She'd have to think about that. For now, though, she nodded. "Anything I can do for you, just let me know."

She faced his cabin, forcing cheerfulness into her voice. "Like chinking. Can I work while you eat?"

He reached for the basket. "Naw. I don't have much left. You'll be missing time with Anna too. Go on back and ask her to show you the meadow of flowers. She'll like to get outside a while."

Patience was being dismissed, but he was right. She should use this time to strengthen her bond with her niece. After all, they should be moving on soon.

Maybe, while they walked to the meadow, she could talk to Anna about when they could leave. Even as she started back to the main house, she had to fight the burn of tears that came with the thought of leaving Jonah Coulter for good.

CHAPTER 10

*A*s Jonah stepped into the barn the next morning, dust motes danced in the sunlight filtering between the boards. One of the broodmares nickered a greeting, but the sound of voices drew his attention toward the feed room and the two figures standing in front of it.

Patsy and Jericho. His brother held his work saddle in both hands, on his way to tack up Pinto for the day, no doubt. When Patsy glanced at him, he couldn't see her eyes well in the shadows, but the tension in her shoulders and the way she gripped her gloves was hard to miss.

After a nod at Jonah, she spoke to Jericho. "I'd like to buy that gelding that I rode here from Missoula Mills. And another, safe enough for Anna to ride if you have one to spare. I'll pay what they're worth." Even her voice sounded worried, though his brother might not pick up the deeper pitch of her voice.

Buy a horse. To leave? So soon?

He should step forward and join the conversation, but his heart had ceased beating, his legs not capable of moving.

That immediate refusal to his suggestion of courting yesterday had knocked him backwards, but when he had time to think through things, he'd planned to see if he could change her mind.

But she was really leaving. She didn't care about him, certainly not enough. He'd been set to give his heart to this woman, and she'd been focused all the time on retrieving her niece and getting out of here.

What did that make Jonah? Her friend, sure. But that kiss... That kiss was what?

Just a temporary amusement.

He tried to swallow, but his throat was too dry.

When would he ever learn?

"You going somewhere?" Jericho's voice was friendly, but the wariness was hard to miss. Patsy had the right to take Anna, but they were all dreading the girl's leaving.

"It's time Anna and I head on. I need to get to Fort Benton and take care of business with my mother's solicitor. We'll plan our next step from there."

Jericho's brow furrowed. "I understand your need to move on, but Fort Benton is a long journey, especially with a young girl. It's not safe for the two of you to travel alone."

Patsy lifted her chin. "I can handle myself. I've made my way in this world for a long time now."

The words twisted like a knife in Jonah's gut. Was this how it would always be? First Naomi, now Patsy, slipping through his fingers, never choosing him. Maybe he just wasn't enough, would never be enough, for any woman to want to stay.

Jericho huffed. "Still too dangerous. Jonah here could go with you."

Two pairs of eyes swung his way, and Jonah swallowed hard, torn. A chance to spend more time with Patsy, to convince her to give him a chance. But could he bear it if, at the end of the trail, she still chose to leave?

Patsy shook her head. "I won't be a burden. We'll be fine on our own."

Right.

He turned on his heel and strode out of the barn.

He needed to think. Needed to hit something.

He strode up toward the house, then turned to go around back where the chopping block was.

Gil and Miles had brought in some logs from a tree that'd come down in the last storm. Jonah snatched up the ax and attacked the first trunk with a vengeance, chips of wood flying.

The steady thwack and sting of the blade biting into the logs grounded him. He poured his frustrations into every swing, bringing home his anger as it sliced through the wood.

Footsteps scuffed behind him, and he tensed. But then he released his breath and swung again. He didn't turn, just kept at it until he'd chopped through the trunk.

As he turned the log face up to split, Eric's voice sounded behind him.

"You all right?"

Jonah paused, the ax blade hovering over the log. He could pretend like all was well, like he didn't care, but Eric had been a good friend these past months. And Eric knew what it was like to lose a woman he loved. Even though that woman had eventually come back to him. Chosen him.

Still…

He blew out a breath, then let his shoulders sag. "Not really."

"She's something special, isn't she?"

Jonah really must have worn his heart on his sleeve if the entire family knew his feelings. He turned to face Eric, and he couldn't help the bite in his voice when he spoke. "She's leaving. Taking Anna and going to Fort Benton. After that, who knows where. Anywhere but here."

Eric's sharp intake of breath clamped fresh guilt over his chest. He should have broken the news more gently. Eric and Naomi had taken Anna into their home. She'd become like a daughter to them. But surely, they'd prepared themselves for this.

"I see." Eric's voice was rough with emotion. He cleared his throat. "I guess we knew it would happen. I'll..." He cleared his throat again. "I'll let Naomi know."

Jonah really was a cad.

He dropped the ax and leaned against the side of the cabin. "I'm sorry. I didn't mean...that wasn't the best way to tell you."

Eric shook his head. "It's all right. It's just...going to take some getting used to, is all. The thought of Anna not being here..." He met Jonah's gaze. "You going with them to Fort Benton?"

A new round of frustration twisted in his throat, and he lifted his gaze to the trees on the back side of the clearing. "I don't know. Jericho thinks I should. I'm not sure." There were so many things he wasn't sure of. Far too many to name.

Eric watched him for a long moment, long enough that his silence made Jonah want to turn and pick up the ax again. Slice through another log.

At last, Eric spoke. "Maybe if you tell her how you feel—"

Jonah flexed his hands. Why had he dropped the ax? He needed something to squeeze if he was going to make it through this conversation. And be honest, anyway.

He didn't meet Eric's gaze. "Tried that. She's leaving. What more can I do?"

"Fight for her." Eric's words came quiet but firm. "Look, I could say I'm sorry about Naomi, but I'd be lying. I'm not sorry —not even a little—because I love her. And when she left me, I didn't just let her go. I searched for her. I hauled my sorry hide halfway across the continent to find Naomi. I hate to break this to you, friend, but I *fought* for Naomi. Maybe I'm a little sorry I had to take her from you, but I'm not at all sorry I got her back."

Eric folded his arms across his chest. "If you really care about Patsy, then you'll prove it to her. Maybe this isn't all about you. You ever think of that? She's obviously wounded, and scared. Maybe she needs a man who's not afraid to prove he's up to the challenge."

The knot in Jonah's middle twisted. Eric was right, probably far more than he realized.

Eric wasn't finished though. "You can hang out here and feel sorry for yourself—that's the safe choice. Or you could show her she matters to you. Show her she's worth the extra effort on your part. A little risk."

Jonah stared at the blurry line of the distant trees. Would it actually make a difference if he went with Patsy and tried to change her mind on the journey? She seemed pretty determined to leave. To have her own life.

If that was what would truly make her happy…

Or you could show her she matters to you. Show her she's worth the extra effort. Did Jonah really think Patsy might be the woman God intended for him? They hadn't even talked about God. Did she even know Him?

That should have been one of the first things he learned about her when he stopped trying to deny his attraction. *Sorry, Lord.*

He'd strayed farther from regular conversations with God than he'd like to admit. Ever since the mess with Naomi when Eric came, it had been easier to let his emotions run loose than to check them and seek the Lord's guidance.

He needed to work on that.

But there was something special about Patsy. Something that came to life inside Jonah when she was near. From that very first moment he opened his eyes to find her pointing a gun at him, he'd been drawn to her in a way he'd never been drawn to another woman. He couldn't put into words what was different about her, but they fit together just right. He could read the nuances of her expressions, could feel what she was feeling sometimes. He'd never been like that with any other person, not even his brothers.

Eric was right. What he had with Patsy was special.

She was special. And worth fighting for.

He met Eric's gaze. "I think I'll go with her."

A slow smile slipped over his friend's expression. "Good. You've got two weeks to tear down those walls. If anyone can do it, my bet's on you."

* * *

*L*ater that day, the afternoon sun cast long shadows across the dirt path as Patience made her way back to the main house from Eric and Naomi's cabin, her heart as heavy as her footsteps. Anna's angry tears still twisted in her belly.

She'd brought cinnamon crisps over as a treat to tell her niece the news, both because she'd seemed to like them before, and because they were the one thing Patience could manage to bake in the cookstove's finicky oven.

But she might has well have brought manure as a gift for all the good it had done.

I don't want to leave. Why can't I stay here with Naomi and Eric? They love me.

Tears had run down Anna's sweet face, her small fists clenched at her sides. Patience wasn't even sure Anna had heard her when she'd said she loved her too. She loved Anna, her only sister's daughter, so much it hurt. She could still remember holding her when she was only a few weeks old. The tiny precious bundle, perfect in every way.

Patience squeezed her eyes shut against the tears.

Maybe...maybe this was a mistake.

No. She forced the thought from her mind.

She *had* to take Anna with her. Hannah would be devastated

if she knew Patience was even considering leaving her daughter with strangers.

Yet Naomi and Eric clearly adored Anna, probably even more than Anna loved them. They were good people, no question there. They could give her the stable, loving home Patience had always yearned for herself.

But she was Anna's blood kin. Family should stay together, shouldn't they? And they would have a nice home once she got her inheritance, then found land and had a cottage built. Maybe she should leave Anna here until she'd built the house, then come back for her.

By then, though, Anna would be even more attached to Naomi and Eric and little Mary Ellen. The tot adored Anna like a big sister.

Patience sighed as she stepped into the clearing where the main house stood. She was doing her best not to let herself think about how hard it would be to leave Jonah. And Anna's resistance was one more weight pushing down on her.

There seemed to be no good answer. Was she being selfish by taking Anna away? Wanting to soothe her conscience? Wanting her own choice instead of what was best for Anna?

She caught the motion of a tall figure striding toward her from the edge of the clearing. Jonah.

She didn't want to face him and his disappointment right now, not when she'd just endured the same from her niece. But she couldn't simply turn and walk away from him.

As he drew closer, there seemed a change in his bearing since the day before. The tension was gone from his shoulders. A freshness marked his expression. Had he forgiven her already? Maybe the thought of her leaving wasn't nearly as painful for him as it was for her.

"I was just coming to find you." He halted in front of her. His blue eyes searched her face, seeing too much, no doubt. "What's wrong?"

She smiled, though it felt brittle. "Fine. I just had to talk to Anna. About us leaving."

Jonah grimaced, understanding softening his rugged features. "I'm sorry."

Patience shrugged, trying to appear nonchalant even as her heart ached. "I knew it would be hard. I'm grateful your family has been so kind to her." She glanced away. Her words made it sound as if she were a stranger, dropping by to pick up her niece after an afternoon playdate. In truth, spending nearly two weeks with his family—with Jonah—had changed her life in ways she might never recover from.

She summoned a pleasant expression with the last bit of self-control she had. "I need to help Lillian with dinner. Dinah wasn't feeling well this afternoon, so I made her promise to let me take over her part when I returned so she could rest."

Jonah's chin dipped, but he didn't step aside. Just regarded her. "I'll be riding with you and Anna to Fort Benton. The cook-stove I ordered should be there now, and I need to pick it up. I'll take the wagon, and that'll make travel easier on Anna."

Patience blinked, her heart stuttering in her chest. She hadn't expected this offer. "You...want to come with us?" She'd thought Jonah seemed angry when his brother volunteered him for the journey. Maybe his change of heart had come with this newfound peace.

Jonah's gaze steady on hers. "I need to go anyway." He hesitated, then added, "And I'd feel better knowing you had some assistance on the journey. It's not an easy road, especially with a child."

She swallowed past the lump in her throat. "Thank you." Having Jonah along would certainly make the trip more bearable. For both her and Anna.

"When do you want to leave?"

"Day after tomorrow, if that works for you." It would give her enough time to prepare Anna and gather the last of their meager belongings. Though in truth, she dreaded it with every part of her.

"I'll be ready." He reached out as if to touch her arm, then seemed to think better of it, his hand falling back to his side. "I'd best let you go help Lillian. Just...let me know if you need anything before we go."

"I will." Thankfully, he turned away before he could see the tears gathering in her eyes.

It was foolish, the hope that rose within her. Jonah was going because he needed to get his cookstove. Maybe he was going *now* because he wanted to make sure she and Anna were safe. But there was nothing more to it than that. She couldn't let herself consider that he might have feelings for her. She couldn't let herself give in to the yearning to stay and make a place for herself and Anna here with the Coulters. With Jonah.

She straightened her shoulders and started toward the house. Time to put regrets behind her and look to the future, whatever it might hold. Jonah and the unexpected haven of his family would soon be just a memory.

But oh, what a bittersweet memory it would be.

CHAPTER 11

*J*onah wiped the sweat from his brow as he lugged
an armload of kindling toward the makeshift
campsite. The day had been a scorcher, not fun
considering they'd sat in the wagon since the sun had still been
a hope on the eastern horizon. Now, a few faint shades of pink
and purple painted the western sky as night prepared to take
over.

Hopefully, tomorrow would be easier. Not just the heat, but
Anna's attitude. The girl had been sullen and whiny all day. She
was hurting something fierce, which tore at his heart. Mostly.
But it irked him the way she took her anger out on her aunt.
Patsy was doing the very best she could, doing what she considered right. He couldn't imagine what he'd do in her position.
Could he stand to let his brother's kids live with strangers
simply because they felt comfortable there? Could he live with
himself if he didn't even try to make a home for them?

No. No he couldn't.

Didn't Anna see how hard this was on her aunt? Patsy had
started the journey trying to talk about the future with her
niece. She'd been all smiles and joy, speaking with optimism he

figured Anna had seen right through. Patsy'd kept that smile for hours, despite her niece's rudeness. But eventually, she'd given up.

Jonah was doing everything to lighten Patsy's burden, but maybe he could talk to Anna after dinner, try to ease some of her pain or at least get her to give her aunt a break.

He dumped his load beside the low flames of the campfire, then dropped to his haunches to add some of the dryer wood he'd found.

Patsy was rummaging through the supplies, laying out provisions for their evening meal.

He scanned the area. "Where's Anna?" She'd been sulking in the wagon when he left for the firewood, but the rig was empty now.

Patsy straightened and turned toward the wagon, her brow furrowed. "Is she lying down in there?"

He'd peeked inside when he'd walked by it a moment before. A knot twisted in his gut. "Anna?" He scanned the trees around, straining for any hint of motion. A few branches swayed and a bird flitted from one tree to another.

"Anna? Where are you?" Patsy strode to the wagon, her voice thick with worry.

It took her only a second to see what he'd already known—that the bed was empty save the two crates of food they'd brought for the journey.

Patsy spun back to him. "Did she go to the creek?"

He started that way, breaking into a jog as he searched his surroundings. There was no sign of the girl at the water. The only footprints in the wet sand of the bank had been made by his own boots when he'd come to get a bucket full earlier.

Patsy ran up and halted beside him, her breath heaving. Her face was ashen, her eyes panicked when they met his. "Where could she be?'

He wanted to reach out and pull Patsy close, to ease her

fears. But they had to find Anna, now. They didn't have much time before darkness would fall, making the search so much harder.

He looked back through the woods toward where they'd left the wagon, forcing his mind to work through the possibilities. She'd been sitting there when he went to search for wood, her arms crossed and her lower lip puffed out.

Angry because she'd wanted to stay at the ranch.

Would she have tried to go back? A girl as young as Anna should be afraid of a journey like that—a full day's ride up and down mountain slopes. Especially after what'd happened to her grandmother.

On the other hand, Anna had survived countless days and nights in the midst of a mountain snowstorm with no shelter. Walking along a clear-cut road must seem easy compared to that other time.

He glanced toward where he'd tied the horses to graze. Would she have tried to...?

Only one bay back showed through the trees. He started toward the animal. Anna was a smart youngster to have taken a horse instead of trying to walk all the way back. Neither of the wagon horses would hurt her intentionally, but they were so big, and little Anna was so small for her age.

Jonah raced toward the remaining horse. Patsy's skirts rustled as she ran behind him.

When they drew near the mare that was still tied, a flash of movement showed in a clearing beyond the trees. His heart seized, and he strained to see in the dusky light.

There was Anna, standing on a fallen log, trying to scramble onto the patient bay's back. Her small hands gripped the horse's mane as she worked to swing her leg over. The calico bag Naomi had sent with her hung from her shoulder.

"Anna!" Patsy half-whispered the anguished cry as she started forward.

Jonah caught her arm. "Let me." Anna was proving desperate, and she might not open up to her aunt as well as she would to him.

At Patsy's stricken look, he softened his tone. "Please. I think I can reach her." He rubbed his thumb over her arm and did his best to show her with his eyes she could trust him. "If I'm not getting through to her, I'll wave for you to come try."

Patsy hesitated only a moment before nodding.

Jonah approached slowly, not wanting to startle the horse or the child. Anna was so intent on her task, she didn't hear him until he reached the gelding's head. Ol' Jasper stood quietly, weary from the long day on the trail.

Anna's jaw dropped when she saw him. He'd expected her to look guilty, but she clutched the horse's coarse mane, her eyes defiant, clear even through the watery layer of unshed tears. "I'm going home." She lifted her chin. "You can't stop me."

Home.

His heart clenched. Was it the Coulter ranch in general she considered home? Or Eric and Naomi's new cabin specifically?

He took a deep breath, choosing his words carefully. "I know you're hurting, Anna. Believe me, I understand wanting to go back to what's familiar. When you have people who love you, that's not something you take lightly. And not something you want to leave."

If anything, Anna's little hands gripped Jasper's mane even tighter, her lips pressing together.

He ducked to meet her gaze a little better. "You know, your Aunt Patsy loves you a whole lot too. It might not feel like it right now, but she wants what's best for you."

Anna's lower lip trembled. "But...I want to go home. I miss Aunt Naomi and Uncle Eric and Mary Ellen."

"I know you do, sweetheart. And it's all right to miss them. But maybe...maybe it would be okay to give your Aunt Patsy a chance. To let her show you how much she loves you." A new idea slipped in. "Does she remind you of your mama at all? Since they were sisters?"

Anna blinked, one shoulder lifting and falling. "Sometimes. When she talks. Her voice is like Mama's."

"That must be real nice, to hear your mama again."

A single tear slipped down Anna's cheek. "I guess so."

Jonah brushed the tear away with his thumb. "What do you say we head on back to camp? It's getting dark and I'll bet you're as hungry as I am. I think your Aunt Patsy packed some of that strawberry jam you like so much. We can spread it on the fresh bread she and Lillian baked yesterday."

For a long moment, Anna didn't move. Then, slowly, she released Jasper's mane and allowed Jonah to lift her down from the log. She leaned into him, her small arms coming around his waist in a fierce hug.

He held her close, a weight pressing in his chest. This child had endured so much in her short life. Losing her parents, then her grandmother, and now being taken away from the home and people she'd come to love.

He would do everything in his power to make this journey easier for her. For Patsy too. No matter how much he hated to lose them both.

* * *

*L*ater that night, Patience gazed into the dancing flames of the campfire, the warmth doing little to chase away the chill that had settled deep in her bones. Anna had finally fallen asleep, and Patience needed a few minutes to sort through her emotions.

The night was quiet, broken only by the occasional pop of the burning logs and the distant trickle of the creek where Jonah had led the horses to drink.

She pulled her shawl tighter around her shoulders, her

fingers twisting the fringe as her mind churned with doubts and uncertainties. The weight of responsibility pressed down on her, as heavy as the darkness that blanketed the camp. Was she doing the right thing, taking Anna away from this new family and home she'd come to love?

The crunch of boots on dry leaves pulled her from her reverie, and she glanced up to see Jonah emerging from the shadows. He settled himself beside her, his solid presence easing a bit of the tension in her body.

For a long moment, he didn't speak, just let her soak in his nearness. This churning inside her needed space to sort itself out. Did she dare share her worries with Jonah? He'd made it clear he wanted her to stay. But he'd not pushed the idea since he agreed to escort her and Anna to Fort Benton. He'd been a help every step of the journey.

He'd been a friend. And that was what she needed most right now.

His voice broke the quiet, its vibrato low and quiet. "Your thoughts are probably burning more fuel than this fire."

A smile slipped out before she could stop it. That image felt right. Her head was clogged with so much steam that she had to release it or else the kettle would squeal.

She let out a sigh. "I'm just...worried I'm making a mistake. Taking Anna away from your family." She swallowed hard, hoping to stop her voice's trembling. "They've been good to her, and she loves them so. What if... What if I'm doing more harm than good?"

"You're doing what you think is best, and that's your job as her aunt. What else can you do?"

A surge of anger flared in her chest. She tossed a dry twig the flickering flames. "But also..." Should she admit this? Did it make her small? Petty?

Probably.

But she needed to say it anyway.

"Part of me is angry at Anna." Even as the words came out, she wanted to snap them back. But the relief of them finally not clogging her throat made her keep going. "I gave up everything for her, so we can be together. Can't she at least go into it with an open mind?"

Shame rolled over her, thick and hot. What was she saying? That her poor seven-year-old niece, who'd endured enough trauma to leave some adults sniveling in bed, should be more grateful? "I'm a horrible person. So selfish. She deserves so much better than I can ever give her." She covered her face with her hands. What must Jonah think of her?

He shifted beside her. "You're not a horrible person, Patsy." His voice was gentle. "And you're certainly not selfish." A long moment passed, but she didn't have the courage to look up before he spoke again. "This whole situation is hard—for her, but for you, too. You lost your whole family, all but Anna. You're doing everything you can for your niece, and that's all anyone can ask."

She glanced at him, his profile illuminated by the flickering firelight as he stared into the flames.

"I think it's pretty normal to be angry when things don't go the way you planned. I was mad at God after all that happened with Naomi last year." He grimaced. "Maybe even before that. Maybe I've been mad at him since Lucy left. Back then, I remember asking Him why. Why He let her go. It never felt like I got an answer. And things just got worse for her. That skunk of a man she married gambled and drank away every penny, so she barely had enough food for her and the kids. Then he got sick and died."

Jonah paused for a breath, then pushed on. "I hoped she'd come home then. I even *prayed* she'd come home." His voice graveled. "But she didn't. Stubborn woman. She stayed right where she was, determined to make it on her own. As if she ever had a chance." He shook his head, his voice taking on a bitter tang. "Instead, Jericho went to check on her and arrived just before she died."

She couldn't blame him for bitterness. Why had God let that happen to such a good family? Was Lucy punished because she'd run off in the first place, against her family's wishes? If that was the reason, Patience had no hope of ever seeing God's good graces. She'd married Michael against her parent's wishes, leaving with him for parts unknown. And surely a gambler was worse than a miner, even a miner who lost all his money gambling.

Silence hung between Jonah and herself, thick enough to clog her throat. She didn't want Jonah to know her own sins, not when he was still dealing with his sister's. She'd rather change the subject. Speak of something lighter. Something more pleasant than the condemnation of a wrathful God.

But before she could find a topic, Jonah blew out a breath.

"There's something else, though. Something I've been hearing about all my life. God's been reminding me of it lately." He sent her a rueful look. "God *does* love us. He created us, and He knew from the very beginning what would happen in our lives. What choices we would make, what hardships would come our way.

His brow creased, and his words came slowly, as if each one were a precious gem, and he was low on cash. "God wants more than anything for us to turn to Him when trials come. He wants us to hide in His protection when it seems nothing can go right. To let Him show us just how much He loves us. He does hate sin, but He's *not* a God of punishment. He's made a way for us to be free, so that when we come to Him and ask His forgiveness, our sin disappears. Then He wraps us in His arms...and loves us." Jonah's shoulders relaxed with those last words. Maybe the thought of God's love took away the weight he'd carried.

But could it be true? Could there be a way for Patience to be free of all her mistakes?

He turned to face her. "I let my anger at God steal away the peace in being His child and the love He's trying to show me." His Adam's apple bobbed. "He has that same love for you. All you have to do is turn to Him. Ask for His forgiveness. Ask to be His daughter so you don't have to fight through life on your own."

Jonah sounded almost like the corner preacher who'd come through Missoula once. He'd talked about God's love and forgiveness. Nice ideas, but if God took a look at the list of things Patience needed forgiveness for, He'd send her off with a *Sorry, ma'am*—if she was lucky.

She summoned a smile. "I'll keep that in mind. Just now, I have my hands full with Anna. I just need to get us to Fort Benton so I can contact my mother's solicitor. He'll tell me the next steps for us." She eased out a long breath. "One day at a time. I've barely been an aunt for most of her life. It's going to take work to learn how to be a decent mother."

His easy smile showed she'd not offended him. "I remember when Lillian and Sean first came to live with us after Lucy died. I didn't know how to handle kids, especially a pair grieving like that. I wasn't a great uncle. Especially not at first." He chuckled. "I'd only had little brothers growing up, and you could just knock them in line when they needed it. Can't do that with a girl."

The thought forced out a short, mirthless laugh. Knocking her in line was one thing her own father hadn't tried. His other methods had worked well enough. "My father found ways to tame my sister and me." Ways she wouldn't be using with Anna.

The weight of Jonah's gaze landed on her, but she kept her focus on the fire. She shouldn't have said that about her father, but something about Jonah made her want to let out the pain.

"Like what ways?" Jonah's voice held that gentle tone again, though steel ran through the core.

Her eyes burned as the memories rose unbidden, the old

hurt as sharp as ever. "I don't know. When I wasn't good enough, he just...put me away. Like I didn't matter." That didn't sound so painful. It didn't capture the way things had truly been.

She pulled up one of the memories. "When I was about five, my mother's cousin and his family came to celebrate Christmas with us. We'd all been looking forward to it for weeks, and I'd been especially excited because they had a daughter my age and I so wanted a special friend.

"Mama had planned a special party for Christmas Eve, and invited several other families. Before the evening began, Father and Mama's cousin were sitting in his office, smoking and talking. I had found an injured cat outside and brought it in. It was struggling to breathe and bleeding everywhere. I knew she needed help, and when I spotted my father, I thought... I carried the cat into his office and set her down on his desk. Blood got on several of his business papers." She had to swallow the knot that clogged her throat as the memory of Papa's face rose in her mind.

"He was so angry. I thought he would hit me. And if he did strike, I just knew he would kill me, right there." Patience's pulse raced, but she worked to slow her breathing. She was grown now. Far away from him. She was safe.

A warm arm wrapped around her, its strength pulling her in, protecting her. How did Jonah know what she needed every time? She let herself lean against him, even let her head rest on his shoulder. It was so strong, so solid beneath her temple. She eased out another breath, sinking into this safety.

He didn't push for the rest of the story, but she needed to finish. She couldn't leave Jonah wondering what had happened that day. "Anyway, my father didn't hurt me. He called the maid to take the cat and had our housekeeper march me straight to my room. They left me there all evening. I could hear the party going on downstairs, the laughing and playing and… And nobody missed me. It was as if I didn't matter at all."

She cleared her throat. "That was just one time, but he always made it clear I wasn't acceptable. I tried but…I was never good enough. Not like Hannah, my sister. She was so good, my parents always loved her."

Jonah's arm tightened. "You were a child, Patsy. A remarkable girl, I'm certain. I'm sorry he couldn't see that. You didn't deserve to be treated that way, no matter how different you were from your sister."

She blinked back the tears that threatened. "I see now that it's not always easy to know the right thing with children. I'm trying so hard to do right by Anna, but I'm scared I'll fail her. I can't be like my father."

Jonah's free hand came up to stroke the hair from cheek, his thumb brushing away the lone tear that had escaped. "I have faith that you won't fail her, Patsy. You love her too much for that." He paused, and when he spoke again, his voice came a little rougher. "She may not realize it now, but she's incredibly lucky to have you. You're going to be a remarkable mother."

His words wrapped around Patience's heart like a warm embrace, easing some of the doubt and fear. This must be hard for him, though, encouraging her to leave, lending his strength so she'd be able to do what he'd asked her not to. Yet he didn't hesitate, just set aside his own feelings and desires for her sake. For Anna's sake.

He truly was a good man. The best she'd ever known.

She should ask him to come with them. Surely there was room in her dream for a man as good and noble as Jonah. The man who'd already taken her heart and seemed to be offering his in return.

But she couldn't do that to him. It wouldn't be fair to tear him away from his family, the ranch, and his new cabin. His roots ran so deep there. She couldn't be that selfish.

So instead, she simply leaned into him, letting his strength and warmth seep into her bones. "Thank you, Jonah." *I don't know what I'll do without you.* She didn't speak aloud the second part, though it pressed deep inside her.

He brushed a gentle kiss on her forehead, the gesture so tender it made her ache. She would have to leave him soon, but for tonight, she could simply treasure his nearness.

CHAPTER 12

$\mathscr{I}$n the swelter of the afternoon sun, Patience swayed with the movement of the wagon, the same steady rhythm she'd felt for just over two weeks now. Jonah said they should see Fort Benton any minute. At last. Already, they were starting to pass a few small houses.

Beside her on the wagon bed, Anna's head rested on a blanket. No wonder she napped during the day, considering she'd cried herself to sleep every night on this journey east, then often been awakened by nightmares. They were what truly exhausted the poor girl. Patience had grown accustomed to waking in the darkness to Anna's crying out, pleading for her parents not to die before succumbing to horrible, horrible sobs. Patience could only wake her, hold her, and cry along with her.

It wasn't fair. No child should have to experience so much loss. Certainly not such a sweet, innocent girl.

Was Patience doing the right thing, taking her away from the Coulters? This new uprooting was clearly pulling up painful memories. Was this giving Anna the chance to truly grieve her grandma? Or was Patience simply forcing her to endure yet another round of grief, this one unnecessary?

How in the world could she ever know the right thing? She wanted to scream with the weight of responsibility. She'd thought she was prepared for this, but how could anybody be?

Jonah called a command to the horses, drawing her attention to the landscape ahead. They'd reached the edge of Fort Benton.

Patience took a deep breath to settle the turmoil inside her as Jonah guided the wagon through the bustling streets. The fort was a hive of activity, people hurrying about their business, horses neighing, and the distant whistle of a steamboat on the Missouri River. It was a world away from the quiet solitude of the trail.

Jonah pulled the wagon up in front of a white-washed respectable-looking hotel, so different from the one she'd stayed in the last time she came through Fort Benton during her trip west. He set the brake and hopped down, then came to the bed where Patience sat beside Anna's sleeping form.

His gaze lingered on Anna. "I'll get us rooms." Then he looked up to Patience. "You'll stay with her?"

Patience nodded, but her mouth felt too dry to speak. Jonah seemed to sense her inner turmoil and gave her a reassuring smile before striding into the hotel.

She brushed a strand of hair from Anna's face. The child still slept, and considering all the noise and hubbub going on around them, that she did so was a testament to how exhausted she must be. So young. So vulnerable. Patience's heart clenched with a fierce protectiveness. No matter how difficult this journey became, she had to believe she was doing the right thing for Anna. She had to.

A few minutes later, Jonah emerged from the hotel and returned to the wagon. "I got us a couple rooms." He kept his voice low. "I'll carry Anna up and unload the bags before I take the animals to the livery."

Patience gathered the bags she could carry, then climbed out of the wagon.

Jonah lifted Anna into his arms. She stirred and whimpered, but he adjusted his hold and pulled her close. "Shh, it's all right," Jonah murmured as he started toward the front door. "I've got you."

I've got you.

To be held, to know somebody *had her.*

It was silly how desperately Patience wished somebody would whisper those words into her ear. Silly and futile.

Brushing the foolish thought away, Patience hurried to open the door for Jonah and his precious load, then followed them inside and up to the second floor.

The room he stepped into was plain but clean with a two-person bed in the center and the usual appointments along the walls—dresser, mirror, chair, and small table.

Jonah laid Anna on the bed, and she stirred. A whimper sounded, then her eyes fluttered open. They flicked around the room and widened. She sprang upright, grabbing for Jonah before he could step back. "Don't leave." She gripped his arm. "Please don't leave me."

He crouched beside her, wrapping a hand behind her little back. "Shh, it's all right. I'm not going anywhere. And Aunt Patsy's right here."

Pain pressed so hard on Patience's chest that she could barely breathe. How had she brought such a brave, strong girl to this condition of terror and exhaustion?

Patience dropped the bags she'd carried and sank onto the other side of the bed, scooting beside Anna so she could rub slow circles on her back, something she'd begun doing every night since this journey had begun. "I'm here, sweetheart. You're safe." It wasn't quite time for the evening meal, so if Anna could sleep a little longer, she would feel better.

Anna's clutch on Jonah gradually loosened, and Patience pulled her niece onto her lap, wrapping her tightly in a hold that should feel secure. Hopefully.

Jonah met Patience's gaze over the girl's head and spoke quietly. "I'll get the rest of our things from the wagon and put the horses up. Then I'll come sit with Anna so you can send those wires you need to."

"Thank you." *For everything.* Her list of indebtedness to this man would fill a book if she were to write it all down. How had she ever thought she could manage this on her own? Where would she be if Jonah hadn't made the journey with her?

He squeezed her shoulder gently before slipping out of the room, leaving Patience alone with her tumultuous thoughts and an overwrought, exhausted child.

Of all the people who could have searched for her after her mother's death, it had been this man. Had God sent him? Was it possible that what Jonah had said the other night was true—that God loved her?

Her mind snagged on that thought and mulled through it. Jonah had said to receive God's love, she only had to ask for His forgiveness for everything she'd done wrong. Then he'd said something else... She worked to find the exact words. *Ask to be His daughter so you don't have to fight through life on your own.*

She knew what it meant to be her father's daughter. It meant rejection. It meant knowing you were never good enough.

If Patience could be forgiven for her faults, for everything she'd done wrong, maybe she *could* be good enough.

Maybe her Heavenly Father would see the injured kitten instead of the bloody rug. Maybe a Heavenly Father could see past the dirty hands and the dirty dress to the heart of a little girl who only wanted to help.

Maybe she'd finally hear that whisper in her ear that she craved—*I've got you.*

Was it really possible to become a daughter of God?

What would that be like? A true daughter of a powerful God certainly wouldn't have to fight and scrape through life. She wouldn't have to look over her shoulder in fear or worry that every kindness might be a manipulation, a bid for control.

Anna shifted in Patience's arms, reminding her of all the ways she'd messed up her life. Not only hers, but now Anna's. This child, who needed to be loved but was afraid, even terrified, because Patience hadn't been a good enough sister or a good enough daughter or a good enough aunt. How could she ever be good enough to be a daughter of God?

She allowed a sigh as she dragged her thoughts back to reality.

She had to keep herself grounded in this world, in the troubles she would face in the next few hours. And days. And weeks. She had to try very hard and do her best to be...to be better than she'd ever been. Maybe this time, this *one* time, she could be good enough. She *had* to be, for Anna.

Which meant there was no time for useless fantasies.

* * *

*T*he afternoon passed too quickly, as Jonah sat with Anna while Patsy sent her telegram. He needed to check at the mercantile to make sure they had his stove ready, so he settled the girls at the hotel's café while he accomplished that errand.

Now, evening had turned to night, and the three of them trudged up the narrow staircase toward their rooms. Johnson had said he would have men available to load the stove tomorrow morning. Which meant Jonah could head back to the ranch tomorrow if he wanted.

Should he? Part of him wanted to stay in Fort Benton every moment he could with Patsy and Anna. Maybe he could still convince Patsy to come back with him.

But just this afternoon she'd been talking about how they

would travel to Indiana. She had all the details planned in her mind. This was what she wanted.

She'd made her choice, and his lingering here would only make it harder on him in the end. She and Anna were safe here in Fort Benton. He would leave money at the hotel so their room would be covered as long as they could possibly need to stay here. Then he'd leave instructions that the remaining money not used be returned to Patsy. That would help a little with their travels.

He swallowed. If only he could do so much more. But she'd made her choice. And he'd not been chosen. Again.

When they reached the second-floor hallway, the dim glow of the lamps attached to the walls flickered against the faded wallpaper, casting elongated shadows that seemed to mirror the heaviness in his heart. At Patsy's door, he turned to face them.

A knot clogged his throat, so he had to clear it before he could speak. "I guess this is goodnight." His chest ached, making the words he needed to say even harder. "I guess I'll be heading back in the morning." The thought of leaving them here twisted like a knife in his gut. He had to change the subject before he said something he'd regret. He dropped his gaze to Anna. Did she realize it was also goodbye? That he might not ever see her again? Was it good for her to know?

She moved to him and wrapped an arm around his waist. "Goodnight, Uncle Jonah."

He wrapped her close and forced out words. "G'night, Anna-bug. I love you." And he did. So much, his heart was splitting.

She pulled back and turned to slip into the room she shared with Patsy. Just like that, she was gone.

He took in air, then let it ease out of him. He needed to focus on the other goodbye now.

Forcing himself to look up, he met Patsy's gaze. He couldn't tell for sure in the dim light, but her eyes looked to be rimmed in red. Her jaw had set firmly in place though.

He studied her face, committing every detail to memory—the graceful slope of her cheekbones, the soft curve of her lips, the way her eyes caught the lamplight and sparkled like stars. "Did you hear back from the solicitor?" He'd forgotten to ask her when he returned from the mercantile.

"I received a wire with his condolences earlier today. He said he'd pull Mama's will and contact me tomorrow with the details." Her voice wavered slightly, and Jonah fought the urge to take her hand, to offer some small measure of comfort.

Instead, he shoved his hands deep into his pockets. "That's good. I'm sure he'll get everything sorted out quick enough." The words felt hollow, so trivial in the face of how his life—both their lives—were about to change. When he rode away in the wagon tomorrow morning, he'd be leaving his heart here in this hotel room. He might never see Patsy again.

He forced himself to meet her gaze once more, doing his best to convey everything he couldn't say aloud. The respect, the admiration...the longing.

Her green eyes glistened, tears welling there but not falling. She would fight every sign of weakness. That stubborn streak was one of the things he loved most about her.

Love.

The word echoed in his mind, taunting him with everything he couldn't have. Everything he was about to lose.

He couldn't lose her. Not without trying one final time. *Lord, help me. Turn her heart.*

He cleared his throat. "You know, you and Anna could ride back with me. If you want to. We could wait another day or two until things are settled with the solicitor." He'd wait here in Fort Benton a year with her, if that was what it took for her to come home with him.

Pain flashed in her eyes, but she shook her head. "I need to see this through." Her voice came out barely above a whisper. "For Anna, and for myself."

Something cracked deep in his chest, a fissure creeping through his heart like a spider's web. His throat burned like desert sand. He swallowed hard, his jaw clenching as he fought to maintain his composure.

With a nod, he forced a smile that felt more like a grimace. "I understand. You and Anna are always welcome. If you ever change your mind, we'll be waiting for you." *I'll* be waiting for you.

Patsy's smile wavered, a single tear escaping down her pale cheek. "Thank you, Jonah. For everything."

He wanted to reach out, to brush away that tear and pull her into his arms. But he couldn't.

Not trusting himself to speak past the lump in his throat, he turned and walked away, his boots echoing hollowly on the wooden floorboards.

He didn't look back. If he did, he might not have the strength to let her go.

As he reached his room, he paused, his hand on the doorknob. The temptation to turn around, to run back to her and beg her to reconsider, was almost overwhelming. But he had to let her go, to let her find her own way.

He pushed open the door and stepped inside. The click of the latch behind him sounded like a death nell.

He leaned back against the door, his eyes closing. *God, I need Your strength to follow through with this. Now more than ever before.*

CHAPTER 13

*P*atience's eyes flew open, heart pounding as she turned to the thrashing figure beside her.

Anna's small form tangled in the blanket, frantic cries surging from her. "No! You can't. No. Oh please, no."

Patience worked the cover off her niece. "It's all right. You're fine. It's all right." She gathered Anna into her arms.

Anna stopped flailing, but sobs overtook her body. She didn't curl into Patience like she usually did after a nightmare, just lay stiff, great heaves surging through her.

"Anna, what's wrong, darling?" Patience tried to rock her, but she seemed oblivious to her comforting.

The sobs came in waves, so much stronger than any other time. Was it because Jonah wasn't here to help soothe her?

Patience pulled her closer, setting her up a little to get her attention. "Anna, what's wrong, honey? What was your dream about this time?" Maybe if Anna talked about it, she could work through the emotions.

Anna's little shoulders heaved as she struggled to catch her breath. "Ma-ma Na-o-mi." The words came out as more of a sob than a name, but Patience couldn't deny what her niece had

111

said. And she'd called her *Mama* Naomi. Usually, it was just Naomi.

She brushed Anna's hair from her wet cheek. "I know you miss her, honey. I'm so, so sorry."

Anna's sobs shuddered through her, impossible to control even as she spoke again. "And Pa-pa E-ric."

Pain pierced Patience's heart as she clutched her niece to her, the girl's heartache palpable in the trembling of her small frame. She had been so focused on attaining her own dreams, her own desires, she'd counted them as stronger than the depth of Anna's attachment to the people who had become her family. Naomi and Eric had given her the love and stability she so desperately needed after the loss of her parents and grand-mother. And sweet Mary Ellen had become the little sister Anna had never had.

Patience had taken her away from that.

And for what? So she could chase after her own dreams?

Even as she pictured that little white house in the wide green valley, she couldn't summon a single thread of desire for it. Not when achieving that picture took her away from Jonah, from the safety in his arms and the way he cherished her.

She'd never felt like she belonged anywhere until she'd met Jonah and gone to his mountain haven. He never made her feel like she had to work harder to be good enough. Even when she was fighting against what he wanted, he supported her. He'd traveled weeks in a wagon over rough mountain roads to help her accomplish what she'd set out to do.

Patience took a deep breath, her decision crystallizing with each heartbeat. "We're not going to leave them, Anna. We're going back with Jonah."

Anna's sobs slowed. She worked to take a breath, but the sobs only allowed short gasps.

"It's all right, my love." Patience murmured into Anna's hair as she rocked her back and forth. "We're going back to Mama

Naomi and Papa Eric. And Mary Ellen and all the people who love you there." She didn't let herself think about what life would look like for Anna when they reached the Coulter ranch. Would she rather live with the people she now considered family? If she did, and if they wanted her...

Of course Eric and Naomi wanted Anna with them. They'd made that clear. Should Patience allow it? If so, then what would she do?

What did Jonah want her to do?

Was she really going to stay at the ranch?

The questions were too many to consider now. The only thing she knew with every part of her being was that they were going back. And they'd better hurry to let Jonah know before he set out. The faint light of dawn was already showing through the window.

Anna's sobs had quieted, but she still clung to Patience, her small body trembling.

Patience brushed a strand of hair from the girl's tear-stained cheeks. "Anna, love. Let's go tell Jonah we want to ride back to the ranch with him."

She pulled back, then wiped her sleeve across her face. They needed to dress, both of them. She'd not unpacked, so there was little to stuff into bags.

Within minutes, they'd both changed into trail-worn dresses, and Patience had quickly refastened her own coif and Anna's braid. Then, she snapped the bags shut and waved Anna toward the door. "Let's go see Jonah."

They stepped into the hallway only to find that Jonah's door was already open.

Patience edged close and peered inside.

The room was empty. The covers had been stretched neatly over the mattress as though no one had slept there in days.

Her chest clamped as her mind scurried to make sense of

this change. Had he left last night? Decided he wanted to be home more than he needed a decent night's sleep?

Tears burned her eyes, and she squeezed them shut. Why had she refused him when he'd asked if they would return with him?

Why had she come to Fort Benton in the first place?

Why, why had she been so selfish?

A small hand slipped into hers, pulling Patience back from her spinning questions. "Where is he, Aunt Patsy? Did he go to get the horses?"

Patience let out a breath, forcing herself to think clearly. "Maybe." Perhaps he had slept here. Perhaps he'd just gotten an earlier start than she'd expected. Was he, even now, at the livery hitching Jasper and Jenny to the wagon?

If not, if he was already gone…

Well, then she was on her own. Which the only way for her and Anna to catch up with him would be to rent a horse. And catch up with him they would, one way or another.

With Anna's hand in hers, she spun toward their room. "Let's get our bags and go see."

Downstairs, the lobby was empty, the clerk not yet at his post. She left their key on the clerk's desk, along with a scrawled note to explain their abrupt departure. She could only hope she wouldn't be dragging Anna back to this place in need of lodging.

She would find Jonah, even if she had to ride all the way back to the Coulter ranch.

With their bags slung over her shoulder, she ushered Anna out into the quiet morning, the first rays of sunlight painting the sky in hues of pink and gold. Where was the livery? She had no idea which direction to go.

A young boy swept the steps of the mercantile a couple doors down, so she called out to him. "Please, can you tell me where the livery is located?"

The lad leaned on his broom and pointed down a side street. "Two blocks that a-ways, ma'am. Cain't miss it."

"Thank you," Patience called over her shoulder, already striding forward as they wove through the awakening town. The town seemed to stretch on forever, each step a painful reminder of how far Jonah might have traveled.

When the livery finally came into view, Patience could barely breathe from running with the bags in her hands.

An older man with a shock of white hair was mucking out a stall near the entrance, but he looked up as they approached, his eyes crinkling with curiosity. "Mornin' to ya, ma'am. What can I be doin' for you and the wee one?"

She sucked in a breath and steadied her voice. "I'm looking for Mr. Jonah Coulter. Did he come to collect his wagon and team earlier?"

The man rested his pitchfork against the stall door, considering her question. "Aye, he did. Left out of here about an hour ago, I reckon."

Her heart plummeted, but she did her best not to show her worries. She would have to go after him. Surely, she and Anna could make up that amount of time. He had a wagon, after all, and they'd be on horseback.

Poor Anna's expression was filled with fear and uncertainty.

Patience had to fix this, for both their sakes.

Squaring her shoulders, she met the man's sympathetic gaze. "Sir, do you have a horse I could rent? My niece and I need to catch up with Mr. Coulter. " Her voice cracked with emotion, but she refused to let the tears fall. Not yet. Not until she'd exhausted every last option. Even if she and Anna had to ride all the way back to the ranch by themselves.

The man scratched his chin. "Well now, I reckon I could loan you a horse. But you could probably jes' walk on over to the mercantile."

"I...I don't understand."

A slow smile spread across the man's face. "Well now, Jonah said he was headin' to the mercantile to load up a new cookstove. Had a few fellas lined up to help him with it. I'd wager he's still there, 'round back with his wagon."

Relief surged through Patience, so strong her knees nearly buckled.

He hadn't left. There was still a chance.

She squeezed Anna's hand. "Did you hear that, love? Jonah hasn't gone yet. We need to hurry."

"Thank you, sir. Thank you so much."

The old man's eyes twinkled. "Git on now with you, a-fore you miss him."

She spun, pulling Anna with her, and they raced back the way they'd come.

Her mind whirled as she tried to picture the layout of the town. There had to be an alley, some way to get behind the mercantile without losing precious time.

There.

A narrow passage between two buildings, just wide enough for her and Anna to slip through.

They hurried down it, reached the end, and rounded the final corner. And there, a beautiful sight lay before them.

The wagon, Jasper and Jenny hitched and ready.

A man stood with his back to them, his hand stroking Jenny's nose as he murmured something. She would know those broad shoulders anywhere, the way his dark hair curled against his neck.

"Jonah!" Anna's cry pierced the morning air as she dropped Patience's hand and bolted forward.

He spun just in time to catch Anna as she leapt into his arms, a wide grin splitting his face as he swung her up and held her close. "Well now, what are you doing here, little miss?"

Patience followed more slowly, suddenly shy, unsure what to

say. She'd already told him no, already walked away from the safety and belonging he offered.

Would he take her back after she'd rejected him? Could he be so simple?

But when his eyes met hers over Anna's head, hope flickered there, along with hesitation. How could he possibly still want her after she'd refused him, over and over? This man loved her far more than she deserved.

He set Anna down gently, though he kept an arm around her shoulders. "Patsy? What are you doing here?" He sounded uncertain, but not angry.

She swallowed past the lump in her throat, daring a step closer. " I was hoping if the offer still stands Anna and I want to come back to the ranch with you." The words came out in a rush. She held her breath as she waited for his answer.

His smile softened. " I would love nothing more than to have you and Anna come home with me."

Home. The word settled into Patience's heart like a long-awaited promise finally coming to fruition.

She moved forward, aching to go to him, to step into his embrace. But she hesitated, glancing at Anna still tucked against his side.

Later. They would have time later to talk, to sort through all that had happened between them. For now, it was enough to know they were going back, and she and Jonah would be able to explore this thing growing between them. She had a feeling this man would move heaven and earth for her. All she had to do was let him.

Anna tugged at Jonah's sleeve, breaking the weighted moment between them. "Can I sit up front with you and Aunt Patsy?"

Jonah chuckled, ruffling her hair. "I think that can be arranged. Though maybe we'll stay an extra few days until your aunt's business is finished. For now though, why don't you climb up while your aunt and I get your bags situated?"

"Okay." Anna scrambled up onto the wagon seat.

Patience watched her, her chest swelling with contentment. This was right. This was where they were meant to be.

She turned back to find Jonah studying her, a soft smile playing about his lips. "What changed your mind?"

She drew in a deep breath, letting it out slowly. "Anna had another nightmare. But this one was about Naomi and Eric and Mary Ellen. When she called Naomi 'Mama,' I realized I was being selfish, chasing after my own dreams when Anna had already found everything she needed." Did Patience dare say more? She had to say at least a part. "I think I might have found what I need too. A new dream."

A tenderness shone in his eyes that made her breath catch. He took a step closer, his hand coming up to brush a stray curl from her cheek. "That makes me happier than I can say." He regarded her another moment, as though working out something in his mind.

She didn't dare speak yet. He needed to decide on his own whatever he was questioning.

Then he took her hand, lifting it to press a kiss to the backs of her fingers. "Miss Patsy Whitman. I know we'll be travelin' together without a proper chaperone." His eyes twinkled a little. "But when we finally reach home, I'd be honored if you'd allow me to court you proper. Show you I'm the man you've been looking for."

She couldn't fight the grin that overwhelmed her face. "I'd like that. It would be an honor."

A bang sounded from within the mercantile, followed by muffled voices. Jonah glanced over his shoulder, then gave her an apologetic look. "I need to help the fellas load that stove, but I'll be back." He squeezed her hand once more before letting go.

Patience didn't trust herself to speak past the emotions clogging her throat. Now she couldn't wait for the end of the journey. She couldn't wait to leave Fort Benton. Two weeks on the trail, and they'd be back at the ranch where it was safe.

CHAPTER 14

*A*s the wagon creaked to a stop in the ranch yard, Jasper nickered hello to the animals in the barn. The ride back from Fort Benton felt like it took a month, but they'd finally arrived. Just in time for the evening meal, probably. Hopefully Sampson was back now too. Surely.

Jonah set the brake and unfolded his tired limbs as he stepped down, then reached up to help Patsy and Anna. The others would descend on them as soon as the first person realized their presence.

Before Patsy's feet even touched the ground, Lillian called across the yard. "They're here!"

The girl's joyful announcement brought half the family spilling out from the house and barn, their faces alight and voices buzzing.

He stepped close to Patsy in case she needed him.

Naomi reached them first, her skirts flapping as she ran to embrace Anna. The little girl leapt into her arms, burying her face against Naomi's shoulder.

"Oh, my sweet girl," Naomi murmured, holding Anna close. "We've missed you so."

Eric joined them, wrapping his arms around his wife and the child they loved as their own. He met Jonah's gaze over their heads, his eyes shining. His expression held as much gratitude as question.

Patsy stood back, watching the reunion with a bittersweet smile.

His chest ached for her.

On the journey back, she had confided that she was considering asking Naomi and Eric to raise Anna as their own. The unselfish notion had filled him with both admiration and trepidation. He'd grown to care for the bright, resilient girl, imagining a future where he and Patsy gave her the loving parents she needed. But he recognized that Naomi and Eric already held that place in Anna's heart.

Perhaps it was his destiny to always be Uncle Jonah, the stalwart support but never the father. The thought left a hollow ache in his chest. Would he ever have a family to call his own?

The rest of the group surrounded them, a whirlwind of hugs, laughter, and questions. Mary Ellen clung to Jonah's leg, gazing at him with her toothy grin. He scooped her up. "Hey there, Cricket. Remember me?"

She studied him with a sly smile, as though trying to decide how to answer. How much did she think about her actions in that two-year-old mind? Then she threw her arms around his neck. "O-nah!"

He held her tight, breathing in her sweet scent and the unbreakable love and trust wrapped up in this little package. He was thankful now that he and Naomi hadn't married, especially since he'd met Pasty. But he couldn't help wishing this precious girl called him Papa. He certainly loved her enough to be her father.

She pulled back and eyed him with a smile as wide as a Montana mountain. "Un-ka O-hah."

Warmth flushed through him like a surging waterfall. Maybe this was better than being a Papa after all.

He tweaked her nose. "My Cricket. I sure missed you. I brought you something back too." He winked, then turned to Anna, back on her feet now that Naomi and Eric had released her. He'd give her the peppermints in a minute, but her adored friend was probably the better gift.

Mary Ellen dove into Anna's small arms, and the older girl gathered her up and began asking questions.

Mary Ellen responded with a babble that made them all grin. "Well."

Jonah turned at his older brother's voice and caught Jericho's grin.

"Welcome home."

He accepted the hand Jericho reached out, returning a smile of his own. "It sure is good to be here." All the months he'd traveled searching for Patsy hadn't felt as long as these four weeks on the trail. Of course, they'd stayed in Fort Benton a few extra days too, as Patsy exchanged telegrams with her solicitor. Better to make sure her part of the business was wrapped up now so she didn't have to return to town.

Jericho's focus slid past him to Patsy. "I'm not sure if I'm surprised you didn't come back alone or not."

Jonah's cheeks heated. He rubbed the back of his neck. "Long story."

Jericho raised an eyebrow, a knowing glint in his eyes. "Not that long, I reckon. Are the two of you...?"

Jonah fought a grin. "I'm going to court her."

Jericho's deep laugh rumbled, and he clapped Jonah on the shoulder. "Let's get you settled. I imagine you're ready for a good meal and a soft bed."

Jonah yawned at the mention of rest.

Patsy stood a few paces away, her arms crossed as she watched the happy chaos of the reunion.

Her eyes met his, uncertainty in their depths.

He started toward her, but a figure emerging from the barn caught him up short.

Sampson. Good.

He ambled toward them, his tall frame slouched and his hands shoved in his pockets.

Jonah turned to Jericho, who'd halted beside him, hands on his hips.

Jonah kept his voice low enough only Jericho could here. "When did he get back?"

Jericho's jaw tightened. "Few days after you left. Said he's been working on a way to sell the sapphires locally so we don't have to take them all the way to New York City anymore."

"Locally? As in, here in the Montana Territory?"

Jericho's expression was grim. "Maybe I made a bad decision not going to New York to deliver a load. Didn't think he'd get worried and take matters into his own hands."

Jonah understood his brother's concern all too well. The sapphire mine had been both a blessing and a burden for the Coulters, a closely guarded secret that could put them all at risk if the wrong people found out.

Sampson reached them, a tight smile on his face as he held out a hand to Jonah. "Welcome back, brother. I see you didn't return empty-handed."

Jonah clasped his hand briefly, trying to read the undercurrent in Sampson's tone. "Patsy and her niece will be staying with us for a while."

Sampson's gaze cut to Patsy, then back to Jonah, a flicker of something unreadable in his eyes. "That so? I look forward to getting to know our guests better."

Jonah had a lot of questions about what Sampson had done in Missoula Mills for so long, but this wasn't the time. Jonah wasn't as concerned about strangers coming onto the ranch as

Jericho was. But if Jericho's tension had anything to do with those men Sampson had been teaching to mine...

Surely not. But what were the odds of him meeting anyone in Missoula who possessed both the integrity and the funds to purchase sapphires?

Dinah approached, little Mary Ellen on her hip. "Why don't we head inside? Supper's nearly ready, and I'm sure you're famished from your travels."

As the family began to drift toward the house, Jonah fell into step beside Patsy. He reached for her hand, lacing his fingers with hers and giving a gentle squeeze.

She glanced up at him, her expression full of emotion.

"We'll figure it out," he murmured low enough for only her to hear. "Together. I promise."

Whatever the future held, he knew without a doubt he wanted this woman by his side.

* * *

*I*t's beautiful, isn't it?"

Patience smiled at Dinah's words. "It sure is." She'd been caught fingering the ornate metal work on Jonah's new stove instead of wiping away food spatters as she was supposed to.

Jericho, Jude, Gil, and Miles had come to help Jonah unload the cookstove and attach the pipes. Then she, Dinah, and Lillian had cooked the first food atop its burners—beans and johnny-cakes. Not a glamorous meal, but it had been Jonah's choice. Both dishes were simple to prepare, so Patience could likely handle them on her own. Maybe someday, she'd cook them here in Jonah's cabin, by herself.

The thought made her neck heat. During the long journey home, she and Jonah hadn't been...affectionate. But they'd talked. He'd told her and Anna stories about things that had happened at nearly every curve of the road.

She'd told them about some of the people she'd met, both on the river boats and here in the Montana Territory.

Jonah had talked about his brothers and the stories of how Jericho and Jude had both met their wives.

Patience had told him and Anna about her childhood, about playing with Hannah and climbing the tree in the backyard and having picnics in the park.

After two weeks on the trail, weeks not filled with fear and nightmares, as they had been on the ride down the mountain, but hope and sharing, she felt like she knew Jonah and his family. She knew far more about them than they knew about her. Even so, there was a shift in how they treated her. Oh, the Coulters had always been friendly and welcoming, especially the women. Yet they no longer treated her as a guest.

Now, it felt like she was one of them.

Dinah had begun talking through each step of her cooking process, telling Patience not only how to prepare each meal but also where they obtained which ingredient.

Lillian promised to show her the best berry patches and which ones to avoid—because apparently, the bears liked them too.

Angela had even become something of a friend, sharing stories of her life back in New York City before she met Jude.

Patience had never experienced this kind of belonging before. She'd always felt like an outsider, even in her own family. She could see now—especially after talking with Jonah that first night on the trip—that her father's rejection had left a deep wound, one she'd tried to fill by marrying Michael, then with the thrill of gambling and the fierce independence of making her own way in the world.

But surrounded by the warmth and camaraderie of the

Coulter family, she'd found something she'd never dared to hope for—a place that felt like home.

When they finished cleaning up the meal, she started to exit the cabin with the others heading back toward the main house. When she realized Jonah wasn't beside her, she turned to look for him.

He lingered at his cabin, his brow furrowed as he studied the wall behind the stove. "You all go on ahead. I'm going to seal around this pipe again, make sure it's good and tight."

"I could stay and help. If you'd like." She wanted to, but would that be overstepping the bounds of decorum? They'd been alone together a great deal while traveling, but that was before they'd been officially courting.

Jonah shook his head, his gaze meeting hers with an off-kilter grin that made her heart pick up speed. " I've got it. It's dirty work, and I don't want to mess up your pretty dress. I'll be at the house in an hour or so."

"Okay, then." She looked away quickly, hiding the blush that heated her cheeks from his off-handed compliment. She'd worn the green paisley that set off her eyes.

She followed the others, stealing one last glance over her shoulder at Jonah's broad back as he knelt by the stove. She couldn't quite name the sensation that washed over her, but it felt suspiciously like the roots of love taking hold in her heart.

Back at Dinah and Jericho's cabin, she helped the others put dishes and leftover food away, then swept the main room before peeking outside. Where was Jonah? Surely, an hour had ended by now. The sun stayed out so late in these summer months that it was hard to tell how much time passed in the evenings.

What else could she do while she waited?

Everyone else had drifted to their own rooms or gone outside to tend to chores. Maybe she should go to the barn and see if she could help. She wasn't above mucking stalls or doing whatever else needed to be done.

When she stepped outside, the sky had grown duskier than she'd expected.

A scent tickled her nose.

Smoke.

She glanced up at the chimney. They'd not had a fire in the main fireplace since she and Jonah arrived back from Fort Benton, and they'd not lit one in the cookstove because they ate at Jonah's new house.

No plume of smoke rose from either opening now.

Which meant...

Her heart thumped as she scanned the forest.

There. From the direction of Jonah's cabin, a cloud of smoke hung low over the trees, acrid and heavy. A sudden, awful certainty filled her. Panic clutched her throat.

"Fire!" She spun and jerked open the cabin door again. "Fire at Jonah's place!"

She didn't wait for a response—she'd yelled loudly enough to wake a hibernating bear. Instead, she turned and screamed as loudly as she could toward the barn. "Fire at Jonah's place!"

Then, she gathered her skirts and ran, her pounding heart matching the frantic rhythm of her feet. Behind her, shouts rang out as the Coulters sprang into action.

She didn't wait for them. Every second mattered. *Please, let him be okay. Please, let him be safe.*

The smoke grew thicker as she neared Jonah's cabin, stinging her eyes and choking her lungs. Flames licked at the roof, the crackling and popping of the fire drowning out all other sounds. The heat hit her like a physical blow, stopping her yards away from the structure.

Several of Jonah's brothers had passed her on the way and reached the cabin before her. They circled the inferno, shouting Jonah's name, searching for any sign of him. But the flames had engulfed the entire cabin.

The walls collapsed with a sickening crunch.

"Jonah!" She screamed, her voice raw with desperation. "Jonah, where are you?"

But there was no answer. No movement from inside. Nothing but the roar of the flames and the anguished cries of his family.

Then Jericho charged forward, just as Dinah screamed. "No! Jericho, no!"

He slowed as he neared the mass of leaping flames. The heat from them must be like a solid wall. Jonah's oldest brother stared inside, raising his arm to his forehead, maybe to protect his eyes from the smoke. With the walls crumpled, he could likely see most of the space. He moved to the left, peering hard as he stepped around a flaming chunk of log. When he reached the corner, he turned and jogged the other way, still straining to see into the cabin's skeleton.

At last he slowed to a halt. His shoulders drooped and he took a few steps back, though he never turned away from the cabin. Dinah moved forward to his side and wrapped her arms around him. The two of them stood there, forms desolate.

Patience focused on the burning ruin, her mind refusing to comprehend the truth. Jonah couldn't be gone. Not like this. Not when they'd just found each other. Not when she'd finally begun to hope for a future, for a place to belong.

Tears streamed blurred her vision. Around her, the Coulters stood in shocked silence, their expressions mirroring the devastation she felt.

Jericho held a weeping Dinah, his own eyes bright with unshed tears.

Jude and Gil stared at the flames, their jaws clenched, while Miles bowed his head, his shoulders shaking.

Patience's knees gave out, and she sank to the ground, a wail of pure agony tearing from her throat. She wrapped her arms around herself, rocking back and forth as sobs wracked her body.

He was gone. The man she loved was gone. The one—the only one who'd seen past her defenses and offered her a glimpse of what a real home could be.

The sobs forced their way out, the pain too great to contain.

She'd kept Jonah at arm's length for so long, fearful of letting him in, of being vulnerable. If only she'd been brave enough to tell him how much he meant to her. If only she'd cherished every moment instead of holding back, always keeping one foot out the door.

Now it was too late. She'd never see his crooked grin again, never feel the strength of his arms around her. Never get to build the life she'd begun to envision for them.

As the cabin collapsed in on itself, the flames reaching toward the darkening sky, Patience let the grief consume her. Let it strip away every defense, every wall she'd ever built.

None of it mattered anymore. The only thing that had ever truly mattered was gone, and she might not survive the breaking of her heart.

CHAPTER 15

*S*moke billowed in thick, black plumes against the gray sky as Jonah sprinted uphill, his heart hammering relentlessly with each gasping breath. The acrid smell of burning timber assaulted his nostrils, growing stronger every second.

That had to be his cabin. How could a fire have started? The cookstove had held no live coals, he'd made sure of it.

His mind raced as his boots pounded the rocky trail. He had been down by the stream, washing his bucket and fetching fresh water, when he spotted the group on horseback, a wagon trailing the strangers as they rode hard away from the mine and the main house.

Instinct had propelled Jonah to follow them, but on foot, he was no match for their speed. That was when he'd seen smoke rising in the distance.

That was when raw panic had seized him.

As he crested the final ridge, he stumbled to a halt, his chest heaving.

The scene before him felt like a nightmare. It couldn't be real.

The cabin was completely engulfed in flames, the wooden beams collapsing in on themselves as they charred and smoldered.

Months of painstaking labor, all reduced to ash and embers. How? How could it have happened? How could he have *let* it happen?

He clenched his fists, fighting back the hot sting of tears. Everything he had worked for, the home he'd been planning to offer Patsy, had just gone up in flames.

"Jonah!" The shout of his name broke through his haze. He turned to see his brothers running toward him. And Patsy.

Jericho, Miles, and the others crowded around him, tugging and hugging and clamoring with questions.

"What happened?"

"Where were you?"

"You scared the hayseed outta us."

Then Patsy was there, launching into his arms.

He folded her in, confused, still struggling to move past the fire. He stared over the top of her head at the smoldering remains. His cabin. Destroyed.

"Thank God you're all right." She pressed her hands to the side of his face, studying him as if she were trying to memorize the sight of him. "Thank God. Thank God."

He got a look at her then, her red-rimmed eyes, the crimson curls that'd come loose from her bun and fell around her face. Her skin was pale, her cheeks blotchy, and she gazed at him with so much love, it almost brought him to his knees.

What in the world?

Jericho must've seen his confusion. He motioned to the plume of flame and smoke behind him. "We thought you were in there."

Oh. She'd thought...they'd all thought he was gone. Burned. Their expressions matched Patsy's—joy and relief shining past red-rimmed eyes.

Jonah's throat pulled so tight that he could barely speak. He forced words out. "Went to the creek." He waved down the slope. "I saw someone. Several men riding hard away from the house or..." He nodded to the remains of his cabin. "I started to chase them, but..." His voice broke.

Gil's eyes widened. "You think they did this? Burned your cabin?"

Realization swept in. Had those men escaped from his cabin? After they'd set fire to it? Why in the blue blazes would anyone have done such a thing?

Cold fury churned in his gut.

He would find out.

His brothers exchanged grim looks, then Jericho spoke up. "We'd better check the mine first. Then we can split up and look over the rest of the ranch." He spun to Eric. "Can you take the women back to our cabin? Stay there until we get back."

Eric nodded, his arm lifting to Naomi's back. "I'll protect them with my life."

Jericho, Jude, Miles, and Gil started downhill.

Jonah had to force himself to turn away from the devastation before him—the symbol of his plans and dreams, still smoking in the clearing.

"I'm so sorry, Jonah."

Patsy's words pulled him from his trance, and he squeezed her arm, then stepped away. "I need to go with them. Figure out what happened here." And make whoever did this pay. He followed his brothers.

"Be careful." Her voice sounded so small and worried that he turned back for a quick look.

She stood with her arms at her sides, alone amid the woods at the edge of the clearing. But she wasn't alone. Dinah and Lillian and Angela had all gathered not far behind her. Eric and Naomi were waiting near the trailhead.

"Stay with the family," Jonah said. "I'll be back." He sure

didn't want her anywhere close to strangers who would burn down a man's brand-new home.

He didn't wait for Patsy's answer, just turned and pushed into a run to catch up with his brothers. There would be time later to process the loss, to grieve what could have been. Right now, he had to focus on finding the men responsible and ensuring they paid for what they'd done.

As the mine came into view, he'd finally caught up with his brothers. But the sight in front of them made Jonah's stomach knot with fresh dread. The door to the shed where they kept filled crates of sapphires stood wide open, the rocks and branches they used to hide the building pushed aside.

Jude approached the entrance before the rest of him. He was the brother who oversaw the sapphires, though they all worked the mine.

Jonah started after him. If anything was missing, Jude shouldn't have to face the loss alone.

At the open doorway, Jude stopped, and Jonah halted beside him. He could barely see anything in the darkness. But that was the problem. They should have a year's worth of sapphires stored here. The last he'd seen, crates had filled more than half the building. And that had been several months before, meaning it should be even more full.

But all that greeted them was emptiness.

"Is there anything left?" Jericho's voice growled from behind. He was the protector of the family. He probably took this blow as hard as Jude. Maybe harder.

Jude stepped inside, his boots scuffing the ground. "About ten crates." Only a couple rows lined the far end.

"God, why?" Jericho asked the question nearly under his breath, but it was clearly a prayer. Not idle swearing.

Jonah drew in a breath and tried to blow out his anger and despair, but they were hanging on. He'd lost his cabin. And now he'd lost the resources to replace it.

He should be praying. He should be turning to God for strength. For wisdom. But his body craved action. And justice. And maybe...revenge. *Help me want to turn to You.*

That was all he could manage right now.

Gil, Miles, and Sampson stood behind Jericho, their expressions a mixture of shock and anger. Gil turned to study the ground around them, and Jericho did the same.

Good idea, looking for clues, but Jonah had seen which way the men rode away. It was time to go after them.

He started toward the house. "I'm going for a few mounts."

"Wait." Jericho's sharp command brought him up short.

He turned to see what Jericho had found, but his older brother was studying Sampson.

"What is it? Spit it out." Jericho sounded like he was about to pull fists on their younger brother. Or something worse.

Sampson dropped to his haunches and touched something on the ground. Then he lifted it in a flat hand, rising to his feet. "This belongs to one of the men I met in Missoula Mills. Trying to cut a deal to purchase the sapphires." His voice held a gravity that showed he knew exactly what this meant.

Jericho took the item from his palm. It sparkled in the moonlight and looked to be some kind of metal or jewelry. A pocket watch maybe. "They must have decided to take what they wanted instead of trading for it." His voice ground out with anger Jonah hadn't heard from him in years.

Jericho clamped Sampson on the shoulder, waiting until he met his eyes. "We'll talk more later about why you brought these vultures to our doorstep. For now, we need to focus. How many? Can they shoot? How well are they armed?"

Sampson swallowed, nodding.

Maybe to give him a minute to regroup, Jericho focused on Jonah. "Get the horses, enough for us all. And all the rifles except two for Eric and the women. Jude, Gil, and Miles, go help him."

Jonah set off at a run, his brothers just behind. They had a long night ahead of them, but they would catch these thieves and scoundrels. Unfortunately, recovering thousands of dollars' worth of gemstones wouldn't make his cabin whole again.

It seemed like every time he was close enough to taste the life he craved, it was jerked out from beneath him.

* * *

Smoke still stung Patience's eyes as she walked with the others back to the cabin. The entire family had shown up—all five of Jonah's brothers, his sisters-in-law, his niece and nephew, not to mention Naomi and Eric and their daughter, plus Anna, who weren't even blood related, but might as well be.

Jonah's brothers had gone with him to check their mine, and she'd heard Jericho ask Eric to stay with the "others" and make sure they were safe. The women and children, he meant.

It irked her to be tossed into a group that made her sound helpless. She might be a woman, but she could likely draw and shoot faster and more accurately than Eric LaGrange. Of course, she shouldn't assume she knew his abilities, just as she wished Jericho hadn't underestimated her.

She let out a sigh. Maybe it was best she stay here and help protect Anna and the others. She sent a glance toward her niece, who walked beside Naomi. The girl's expression was so somber, her eyes almost hollow.

Naomi held Mary Ellen, who'd been fussing since they arrived at the fire. Perhaps the tot knew something was terribly wrong, or maybe she was simply hungry. Either way, Naomi had her hands full soothing her.

Eric, too, seemed occupied speaking with Dinah and Angela in tense tones. Something about the fire and...a mine?

Whatever it was, it wasn't Patience's business. She moved in close to Anna and rested a hand on her shoulder. "Everything is fine, you know. Jonah and the other men have just gone to check on things. We're all safe."

Anna nodded, but her gaze remained fixed on the dark trees before them.

Her heart ached for the girl. If only she could take away her fear and uncertainty. But how could she reassure Anna when her own thoughts were a tangled mess of worry and frustration? She should be out there, helping Jonah and his brothers, not stuck here feeling useless.

As they reached the cabin, Patience held the door open for the others to file inside. The space felt cramped with so many people, the air heavy with unspoken fears. Naomi settled into a bench seat by the hearth, Mary Ellen on her lap and Anna at her side. She was speaking in quiet murmurs to the girls, and the magic of her voice already had both children smiling a bit more than before. If only Patience could have had that same effect.

Angela, Lillian, and Dinah had moved to the kitchen, and already the scent of warming stew filled the air, a comforting aroma that almost made her forget the smoke that still clung to her dress.

Eric and Sean were traipsing inside and out, hauling firewood and water. The others ate in shifts, each filling a bowl when they were ready for it.

Patience stepped to the window, out of their way, and peered out into the night. The moon had risen fully, casting an eerie glow over the landscape. Shadows seemed to lurk around every corner. She couldn't stomach the thought of food just now. Not with what happened to Jonah's cabin, and now he was out searching for the men who had done such a cruel act.

Minutes crawled by with agonizing slowness. Eric had joined his wife and the girls near the hearth and was now reading to them.

Sean sat nearby, whittling the horse he sometimes worked on in the evenings.

Her nerves wouldn't let her sit, but she did her best to confine herself to watching at the window. Jonah was out there, facing God knew what danger, and here she was, standing uselessly.

She could take it no more. She had to do something, anything, to help Jonah and his brothers. She hurried into her bed chamber and snatched her derringer from her satchel. She'd stopped wearing it in her sleeve, but she needed it now.

After adjusting it so she could flip her wrist and draw, she returned to the main room. Maybe she should tell the others she was headed out, but they would try to stop her. She could fend for herself out there, and if she had to loiter here in the cabin another half hour, she might go mad.

So she strode across the cabin, keeping her steps light. Nobody looked at her, so she slipped out the door and into the smoky night air. In the barn, the familiar scents enveloped her. A horse nickered softly, and she made her way down the aisle until she found the gelding she'd ridden from Missoula Mills. She ran a hand along his neck, feeling the warmth of his coat beneath her palm. "Hey there, old friend. Looks like we've got another adventure ahead of us."

The saddle felt heavy in her hands as she lifted it onto the horse's back, the leather creaking as she tightened the cinch. The last time she'd ridden this horse was when she first came to this ranch. She and Jonah had been strangers, and she'd not been certain at all she could trust him. So much had changed since then. Not only did she trust him, she was ready to risk her life for him.

She swung into the saddle, and the horse took a step forward, as eager to set out as she was. She nudged him with her heels, and the gelding moved into a brisk walk. She aimed him toward a trail she'd noticed before, one that looked heavily traveled and went the direction the brothers had ridden. This must lead to the mine she'd heard mentioned.

The path wound through the trees, and in the dark, she had to focus on the packed dirt so she wouldn't lose the route. Branches reached out like gnarled fingers, catching at her hair and clothes. The farther she rode, the more the shadows closed in around her.

She strained for any sounds that would signal the presence of the Coulter brothers—the murmur of voices, footsteps through the dried pine needles. Maybe even a whistle to catch her attention if they spotted her first.

But no sounds came.

Maybe she should turn back.

They'd not had horses, so if they planned to go after the arsonists, they would need to come back to the barn for mounts. She should have thought of that and waited for them instead of setting out alone.

Foolish, overconfident girl.

Just as she was about to rein her horse around, a flicker of light ahead caught her eye. She reined in her horse and peered through the trees at the dying coals of a campfire, the embers still glowing. Someone had been here not long ago.

CHAPTER 16

atience edged her gelding closer, scanning every part of the small campsite for signs of life. The place looked empty. When she was certain she was alone, she nudged her mount into the tiny clearing so she could get a better look. Maybe whoever'd been here had left something behind that would identify them.

A horse snorted behind her, and Patience whirled around.

A shadowy figure on horseback emerged from the trees, and her heart leapt into her throat. In one swift motion, she flicked her wrist and slid her derringer into her palm, the metal cold against her skin. She aimed it at the approaching silhouette.

"That's close enough." Her voice sounded far more confident than she felt.

The man lifted his chin, and moonlight shone on his face. Recognition hit her like a physical blow.

It was *him*—Douglas, the ruffian who'd accosted her by the stream that day. The one who'd threatened her...and whose eyes now held cold malice.

He regarded her with a sneer. "Well. If it ain't the little lady who don't know when ta keep her mouth shut. Thought you'da learned your lesson last time."

Patience kept her gun trained on him, even as her pulse pounded in her ears. "Was it you? Did you set fire to Jonah's cabin?"

Douglas let out a harsh laugh. "Maybe I did, maybe I didn't. Ain't none of your concern."

"It is my concern when you threaten people I care about." Her finger tightened on the trigger. She would have to shoot him. She'd have to kill this man before he had a chance to gain the upper hand. Maybe she could get an answer first. "Why? Why are you doing this?"

His horse shifted its weight. Was he moving closer? A dangerous glint sparked in his eye. "You're a dumb one, ain't ya? Shoulda killed you last time I had the chance. Would've saved me this trouble now."

Fear coiled in her belly, but she held her ground, her aim never wavering. "Tell me why. Are there others? What do you want with the Coulters?"

In a flash, his horse lurched forward while he ducked low.

She pulled the trigger, but her shot missed high.

He wrenched her wrist. Pain lanced through her arm, and the derringer fell from her grip. She slammed her heels into her gelding's side to keep distance between her and this man, but he'd already grabbed her reins.

She pulled her leg up to leap from the saddle, but he grabbed her arm, his grip a vise around her. His fingers dug into her flesh as he yanked her from the saddle.

She hit the ground hard, her hip and ribs bearing the brunt of the impact and knocking the wind from her lungs. She fought to suck in air, even as a single thought speared through her mind.

Run!

She rolled to her hands and knees, pushing herself up with

one hand and using the other to fumble for the knife she kept in her boot.

But Douglas crashed down on her, slamming her belly to the ground. His weight pinned her, making it impossible to breathe. Then his hands closed around her throat, cutting off her air. She clawed at his fingers, panic exploding as black spots danced in her vision.

"I'm gonna finish what I started." His voice sounded so distant. "And this time, I'll make sure there ain't nothin' left of you to find."

Darkness crept in at the edges of her sight. She was too weak to fight him. Too weak to defend herself.

This couldn't be how it ended. Not here, at the hands of this madman. She'd fought too hard, come too far. Jonah...Anna... they needed her.

Even as despair threatened to pull her under, a single thought crystalized in her oxygen-starved mind.

God, help me!

Only a miracle could save her now.

* * *

The gunshot split the night air, sending Jonah's pulse surging.

"That wasn't far away." Sampson whispered. The two of them had been out searching for more than a quarter hour, but maybe they'd finally found their target. Or some of their other brothers had. They'd all ridden out in pairs.

He spun his horse in the direction of the shot and pushed the animal into the fastest trot he could manage while weaving through all these trees. His heart thundered, even as he tried to think clearly. What if the others had found trouble. Would there only have been one shot? Maybe it had been a signal that they'd discovered a clue.

As they neared the source of the sound, he reined down to a walk so they moved quieter. Just in case.

Noises drifted from ahead. Were those grunts? And a man muttering? It sounded like a fight.

Jonah reined in his horse and grabbed his rifle. He lowered to the ground, then looped his reins over a branch, whispering, "We'll be quieter on foot."

Sampson joined him, and they crept toward the noises quickly. Someone might be in trouble. Had one of the strangers gotten the drop on a pair of his brothers?

Had that shot been the sound of Jericho being murdered? Or Gil? Or Jude?

If so, then the brother who remained would surely fight to the death. But what if it was the youngest, Miles? He'd have little chance against a grown man, likely a seasoned thug who wouldn't hesitate to fight dirty.

They reached the edge of a small clearing, and Jonah slowed to peer through the branches.

As he focused on the scene, his breath caught.

A man knelt over a prone figure…and even in the darkness he could make out the familiar rich green skirt.

Patsy.

She lay facedown, and the man had his hands wrapped around her slender neck.

Rage surged through Jonah, propelling him forward.

He lunged at the attacker, a roar tearing from his throat as he ripped the man away from her.

They crashed to the ground.

The man recovered, propelling them into a roll the attacker put him on top. He reared back and aimed a punch.

Jonah dodged it, slamming a fist into his enemy's cheek, but a return blow struck his nose, and the crack radiated through his head.

His eyes watered, but he struggled through blurred vision.

Pushing himself up to face his adversary who was preparing another attack.

Before he could react, Sampson intervened with a strong pull, yanking the attacker off Jonah.

Jonah gathered his strength to help his brother, despite the throbbing in his nose. Together they could pin him down.

Patsy.

Was she alive? Or was he too late?

Let Patsy live, Lord. Please.

Maybe he moved too slowly.

Maybe the broken nose had dulled his instincts. Before he could focus enough to see the man on the ground, Sampson shouted.

Metal flashed in the dim light, and Sampson fell back, twisting onto his side, away from the man.

Jonah honed his focus on this vile man who seemed to have more lives than a cat.

The cad brandished a knife, fisting it high, its bloody blade aimed at Jonah. "Don't move or you'll be the next to die."

Next?

Who was dead? Sampson? Patsy?

"I'm a perfect aim with this blade," the enemy said, his chest heaving as he struggled to catch his breath..

Jonah pushed his fears aside. He had to be smart about this next move—it might be his last. It had to be the one that stopped this murderer forever.

This guy was familiar. The last time Jonah saw him, they'd fought in the dark. Except that time, the scoundrel had skulked away into the forest.

Douglas.

Jonah should have killed him then.

Surely Sampson hadn't been working with him?

Didn't matter. Right now, he had to get them all out of this.

Sampson lay curled on his side, cradling his arm, blood soaking his hand. Which mean he was alive.

Did that mean Patsy was dead?

He couldn't see her, nor could he hear her breathing.

God, please...

If only he'd spent more time with the Almighty. Then this wouldn't be simply the desperate plea of a man who had nowhere else to turn. God would be accustomed to hearing from him. Maybe He'd be more willing to hear and help.

Please, Lord. Don't hold my sins against her. Save her so she has a chance to turn to You. I'll do a better job of telling her about You.

Patsy had seemed to know so little about God. Jonah might be the one God had brought into her path to bring her to faith, and he'd only had the nerve to speak of Him one time.

I'm sorry, God. Please. Give me another chance with her.

The man shifted, drawing Jonah's focus back to the present.

Jonah needed a weapon. His rifle probably lay somewhere near the spot where he'd knocked the man off Patsy. Could he reach it? He didn't dare turn and look. He couldn't risk provoking the man, not with Sampson bleeding out and Patsy...

Don't think about that. She was in God's hands now. *Please, Lord.*

The killer's malicious eyes darted between Jonah and Sampson. "Looks like your brother ain't doin' so well." His mouth curled into a cruel grin. "That means you're next. I shoulda killed you before." The man shifted to his feet though stayed in a crouched position. "I'll get it done now."

Sampson groaned, drawing the man's attention.

Jonah reached behind him, doing his best not to move so much the enemy noticed. If he could just touch metal...

The unmistakable click of a gun cocking shattered the tense silence.

"Don't move." Patsy's voice rang out, hard as steel.

Jonah's heart leapt. He risked a glance in her direction. She stood in the shadows, his rifle aimed steadily at their attacker. Even in the darkness, Jonah could see the determined set of her jaw.

She was alive. And fierce. And so beautiful it made him want to weep.

He shifted his gaze back to the man, whose surprise morphed into cruel amusement. "You don't have the guts."

"Try me." Patsy's tone didn't waver.

The man's gaze darted between Patsy and Jonah. His fingers flexed on the knife.

Jonah tensed, ready to intervene if necessary. He wouldn't let this killer get near her.

In a blink, the man spun and lunged toward her.

A blast split the air. The killer jerked. His expression changed to shock, his eyes going wide as he was thrust sideways by the impact of the bullet. He lurched through the air, and as he struck the ground, his head flopped, then dropped forward, his nose touching the ground.

His body stilled.

Jonah blinked, sucking in a breath as he stared at the lifeless body.

The man was dead. At least, it certainly looked that way.

Patsy. He pushed to his feet and turned to her.

She lowered the rifle, her chest heaving. Their eyes met, and the steel lacing her eyes melted into relief. "Jonah."

CHAPTER 17

*J*onah crossed to her in two long strides, pulling her
into his arms. ""Are you all right? Are you hurt?"

"I'm okay." She looked past him. "Your brother."

He spun to where Sampson still lay curled on the ground.

Patsy strode forward and dropped to her knees by his side.
"Can I see it?" She pulled Sampson's wrist forward to get a
better view of the gash across his lower arm.

The mass of blood made Jonah's middle churn, and he forced
his gaze away to gather his wits. They needed to get Dinah and
her doctoring skills.

But first, he should check the man lying motionless, the one
who'd done all this damage and likely a great deal more. Make
sure he would never again lift his hand to hurt someone Jonah
loved. And where were the others he'd seen riding away before
he discovered his cabin ablaze?

Jonah crouched and flipped his body over, the lifeless eyes
telling him all he needed to know. But he felt for a pulse in his
neck anyway.

Nothing.

He turned to help Patsy, his mind catching up with all that

had happened, though the throbbing in his nose made it hard to focus. Eric had broken his nose a year before, and Jonah recalled too well the difficulty of recovering from this particular injury. He swiped blood dripping from his jaw, the least of his worries, as he crouched beside Patsy. "What can I do?"

Should he send Patsy to get Dinah? He couldn't let her go by herself though, not with the possibility of dangerous men still lurking in these woods. They would have to bandage Sampson as well as they could, then take him back to the house.

Patsy had already tied a strip of green cloth around Sampson's bicep. The fabric dug in, nearly disappearing in the crease of his shirt, but the flow of blood had slowed. Patsy wrapped a second strip of fabric around the gash to act as a bandage. "I'm not sure if this is right, but I'm trying to stop the bleeding. We need to get him back to the house."

She sounded worried, though she was doing everything he knew to do.

He touched Sampson's shoulder. "Can you sit a horse? We've got to get you back to Dinah."

His brother's skin was so white that it practically glowed in the moonlight. His eyes were squeezed shut, but he gave a small nod. "Yeah." The word came out like a grunt.

Jonah straightened and looked around to get his bearings. They'd left their horses tied not far away, and the animals should still be there. Sampson could ride double with him.

He pushed to his feet, but the distant sounds of hooves through the forest stopped him up short.

He spun to find a gun. These riders might be his brothers—but they might not.

His rifle lay where he'd thought, near the spot where Patsy had almost died. He scooped it up and strode forward to wait where he could see through the trees. With the rifle stock tucked in his shoulder, he kept every sense alert. A quick glance back showed Patsy had picked up her rifle again and was coming to join him.

"It might be my brothers." He spoke just loudly enough for her to hear.

He'd like to tell her to hide behind a tree until he knew they were safe, but she'd proved she could hold her own as well as he could. He wouldn't try to force her into the shadows so he could play the hero. All he could do was pray God kept her safe.

Please, Lord.

The noises grew louder, and finally two riders emerged from the shadows.

Jericho. And Miles.

Jonah lowered his gun as he let out a long breath. "Over here. Hurry."

He and Patsy moved back into the clearing as his brothers reined in. Jericho took in the scene, his focus stalling on Sampson's curled body. "What happened?" He leaped to the ground and strode toward their little brother, even as his gaze locked on Jonah.

"It's a knife wound. He's lost a lot of blood, but Patsy tied off the arm. We need to get him back." Facing Miles, Jonah motioned toward the tied horses. "Go get our mounts. They're tied just out of sight." That way he could quickly bring Jericho up to speed.

Jericho knelt beside Sampson, his demeanor turning almost tender as he rested a hand on his shoulder. "How you doin', Sam?"

He managed a pained smile. "Fine."

The two had nearly come to blows an hour ago, but surely Sampson could feel the unconditional love in Jericho's greeting. They were a family, no matter what mistakes they each made.

Jericho ran a hand over Sampson's hair as his gaze roamed the injured arm. "Dinah will be tickled to have someone to doctor."

His gaze lifted to take in Patsy. She was disheveled, but she looked...strong. With a nod to the dead man, Jericho said, "He hurt you?"

She shook her head. "I'm all right." Her voice rasped, probably from that monster choking her.

Jericho surely heard it, but he only frowned at Patsy, then rose. He turned and stared down at the body for a long moment, his jaw hard. "Who is he?"

Before Jonah could answer, Sampson spoke. "Douglas." His voice sounded tight and strained. "He joined on with...those men...after I...met them."

Jonah stared at his brother. Maybe this man was connected to the others, but maybe his presence here at the same time as the sapphire thieves was coincidence. "Actually, Patsy and I first saw him in Missoula Mills. He was cheating at the card table and tried to start trouble. Then he attacked Patsy on our way here. He ran off when he realized he was outnumbered. He might have come for revenge."

But had he stolen sapphires too? And burned down the cabin?

Where were the other men Jonah had seen earlier?

Miles led the two horses into camp.

"Let's get you home and patched up," Jericho said. "We'll figure out the rest later."

Together, Jericho, Miles, and Jonah hoisted Sampson onto Jericho's horse so he could hold him steady for the ride back.

Jude and Gil arrived, summoned by the gunshots.

Gil had managed to catch Patsy's horse, though not another that'd been running alongside it—Douglas's, if that actually was the man's name.

The brothers draped his body over Sampson's mare, and at last they were ready.

Jericho took charge, as always. "Miles and Gil, ride ahead and let Dinah know we're coming."

The two disappeared into the night, and the rest of them started at a slower pace. Every grunt of pain from Sampson made Jonah's gut clench with worry. *Hang on, little brother. We'll get you help.*

A glance at Patsy on her own mount showed her face paler than usual. Yet her expression still held that strength she always possessed. She would struggle in the coming days with the fact that she'd killed a man. Everyone did. Taking a life was no small matter, even in self-defense. But Jonah would be by her side through whatever they had to face.

And his cabin. Exhaustion weighed his chest again as the image slipped in of that blackened smoking skeleton. He would rebuild. He wouldn't let this loss take him down. But maybe... maybe he and Patsy could plan the new version together. If she'd have him.

He'd wait to ask until she was ready. But he wasn't letting her go again. Every part of him knew this was the woman God had created for him. His perfect match. A blessing he'd given up hope of ever receiving.

But God had a much better plan than Jonah had ever imagined.

* * *

The morning light filtered through the curtains behind Sampson's bed, casting shadows on Jonah's brother's face as he lay propped up against pillows, his arm wrapped in bandages. Though still pale, a hint of color had returned to Sampson's face after a night's sleep.

He'd stayed in Patsy's room—the spare bed chamber in the main house. Patsy had moved up to the loft with Lillian so Dinah could have ready access to Sampson throughout the night.

Now, the rest of Jonah's brothers gathered around the bed to talk through all that'd happened the night before. What a nightmare it had all been, but at least they'd lived through it, which was more than could be said for Douglas. They'd searched around the camp and found no other clues, though it appeared several men had camped there.

Jericho cleared his throat. "We need to figure out who took the strawberries and what our next move is."

Jonah nearly rolled his eyes at the code word they used for the sapphires. Everyone here knew what they mined, even Patsy after last night. But this was a habit Dat had insisted on so they wouldn't slip up and name the gems around strangers.

Jonah perched on the bed. "Tell us about the man—Douglas. You're certain it was him?"

Sampson nodded. "I took another look after we got here last night. I'm sure." His voice sounded strained, like even talking used up a lot of his strength. "He joined up with the others a couple days after you left Missoula Mills."

"He must have gone straight back to Missoula after he attacked Patsy by the creek."

"You mentioned that last night." Jericho turned to Jonah. "Tell me exactly what happened there."

Jonah did, starting with the ruckus the man made in the card room and ending with him fleeing into the woods after Jonah and Patsy fought him in the water. If only Jonah had given chase then, not let the man escape to do worse damage later.

How was Patsy coping today with the shock of it all? She'd been so pale last night. Brave like always, but he'd seen her fear too. If only he could wrap her in his arms now, somehow shield her from the aftermath of what had been done to her and what she'd been forced to do to save them all.

She'd still been sleeping when he came up the hill from the bunkhouse, but maybe she'd be awake when they finished this meeting.

Jericho turned back to Sampson. "And you met Douglas when?"

Sampson took a slow breath and blew it out. "I spent a day teaching the fellows to sluice mine like I'd told Jonah I was doing. Douglas joined us the second day. I thought he looked familiar, but I didn't realize he was the man who caused trouble in the saloon." He shot a look at Jonah. "I wasn't paying enough attention. I should've known."

Jonah dropped a hand on his shoulder. "It's all right."

By Sampson's expression, he didn't agree, but he continued. "Anyway, as we were working, the other two mentioned they were learning to sluice mine so they could get on with an outfit owned by a man named Mick, that he was paying fifty percent of earnings to anyone who worked with him. He supposedly had this amazing place where he was mining for high quality gemstones and raking in the profits."

Sampson's brow furrowed. "I asked to meet him. After I'd worked with those fellows for a few days, they took me on to Helena, where Mick had a house. We found him in a cafe. They introduced me, and he invited us to join him for the meal."

He shook his head. "I just listened to the others talking to him and could tell the man knew the business and had connections with retailers in the east, just the way our usual buyer in New York does. It was clear during the meal that the fellows I was teaching were itching to get on with this Mick, and by the way the folks in town treated him, like he was the mayor or some sort of boss... I'd say the guy has power.

"When we were finished, I walked with him to the telegraph office so I could talk to him alone. I asked if he ever purchased gems locally in bulk, things like sapphires or rubies. He said absolutely and that he hoped one day to be the largest exporter of precious stones."

Sampson's gaze drifted to the bureau in the corner, though his mind seemed far away, as if he saw the memory play out. "I asked what price he would pay per crate for high grade sapphires. He quoted a price just shy of what we got last year. I figured, working with him, we wouldn't have to pay for transportation all the way to New York. I figured to come back and talk to you about it, Jericho. I'd agreed to meet the man again in two months' time."

Jericho's jaw tightened. "And then he sent his men to follow you home and take the sapphires without paying for them."

Gil spoke up. "Or maybe this Mick didn't do anything, and those other men you taught to sluice mine came up here on their own." He raised his brows as he waited for Sampson to comment.

Sampson squinted and paused a moment before answering. "I don't think so. I got the feeling none of those men moved without Mick giving the order to."

A heavy silence filled the room.

Jonah's stomach churned with a mixture of anger and dread. How could they possibly go up against a man with that much power and resources?

Jericho finally spoke, his voice low and determined. "Do you have any idea who the men were who came? How many would have come?"

Sampson looked almost as weary as he had last night. "That pocket watch belonged to Thompson, one of the men eating with Mick when I first met him. I think he might be a foreman or something in the operation."

Jericho turned to the rest of the brothers. "Several of us need to go to Helena, to find this man Mick."

"No." Sampson's single word was loud and vehement. "He has a lot of men and a lot of power. There's no way five or six of us could get the upper hand. Even if we found a lawman and got him involved... I don't think we're getting the sapphires back."

Jericho scowled, his lips pressed closed.

The tension in the room was thick and heavy while the rest of the brothers waited to hear what the oldest would say.

"We'll think and pray about it, then meet again tonight. Probably several of us will go scope the situation out, but let's pray before making a decision."

As they began to disperse, Jonah left the room with a restless energy thrumming through him. As concerned as he was about the mine and the sapphires—more importantly, the men who had burned his cabin down—he was more concerned about Patsy.

He had to see her.

CHAPTER 18

$\mathcal{A}$s Jonah walked through the cabin's main room, Dinah and Lillian worked in the kitchen. Jericho stopped to talk with his wife while Jude, Gil, and Miles filed outside to get on with the day's work.

Where was Patsy?

He started to approach Lillian to ask if she'd come down from the loft yet, but a quiet voice drifted in from outside. Gil's teasing tone answered, raising Jonah's hackles a little. Of course his brother could talk to Patsy, but the childish part of him had wanted to be the first one to see her this morning. The first to look into her eyes and see if darkness lingered there.

He reached the doorway in three long strides and stepped outside, squinting against the bright sunlight.

Patsy was walking to the house with a basket in her hand, but she stopped when she saw him. They stood a few steps apart, her gaze meeting his. "Morning." Her voice came soft, heavy with fatigue.

"Morning." He itched to reach for her, to pull her into his arms and hold her close. But he wouldn't overwhelm her. "How are you feeling?"

She shrugged, her gaze drifting away. "I'm all right. Just tired."

"Did you sleep well? I wasn't sure after..." Was it better to bring up all the hard events or wait for her to do so?

She looked back at him, her expression turning wry. "Sure. Like a baby."

He didn't miss the playful sarcasm. In her defense, it had been a stupid question.

She shrugged. "I'm not sure I slept at all, to be honest."

He nodded. "Understandable."

This was too awkward, standing by the stoop, trying to have a serious conversation. He needed to spend time with her. He also needed to go see what was left of his cabin. Would that be hard for her to see? Probably. It'd be hard enough on him, yet having her there would make the loss easier to take.

He nodded that direction. "Would you like to walk with me? I'm going to see what can be salvaged."

Her gaze turned uncertain, yet there was a spark of interest too. "Let me just take this basket inside."

Jonah waited, his heart thumping. He wanted to be strong for her, to help her through the aftermath of last night. But he longed for her comfort too. Did that make him weak, or just human?

She emerged a minute later, her expression a mix of determination and vulnerability. They fell into step, heading down the hill. The sun was already turning hot, but Patsy wrapped her arms around herself.

She looked so fragile. He needed to find a way to broach the subject of last night.

He cleared his throat. "Do you want to talk about it? About what happened?"

She glanced at him, her eyes shadowed. "I don't know what to say. It all feels like a nightmare."

He nodded. "I can only imagine, the way that man attacked you." A fresh round of bile churned in his belly. "I'm so sorry I didn't stop him that day at the creek."

Her steps slowed, and she turned to face him. "You saved my life, Jonah. Both at the creek and last night." She swallowed hard. "It was a miracle, the way you showed up just in time."

His heart pounded. Was God creating an opening for him to share his faith? "I think so too. You know God sees you. He's there, even when we don't cry out to Him."

Something like a smile slipped into her eyes. "I did pray for help. When that man had his hands around my neck, I knew nothing could save me except a miracle. I prayed for help." She frowned. "I didn't pray out loud, though. Does that matter?"

Joy wove through him, and a smile lifted his tired muscles. "He knows our thoughts. He heard you. And He saved you."

"Yes, He did." But she looked away, blinking rapidly. "I just wish I didn't have to kill…"

"I know." He touched her arm. "You did what you had to do to save us all. I'm grateful God gave you that strength. I'm grateful you were so brave. I'm grateful for *you*."

She met his gaze again, her eyes bright with unshed tears. A single one broke through her barrier and slipped down her cheek.

He brushed it away with his thumb, letting his hand linger against her soft skin. His pulse picked up speed. Just the feel of this woman brought all his senses to life.

She must have felt the same, for she leaned into his touch. Her eyes…those eyes drew him body and heart. At the moment, they held so much turmoil, yet there was an inner strength. A solidness that shone through even during this hard time.

"Patsy…" He swallowed the emotion that rose. "I don't know what I would have done if we hadn't gotten to you in time." His voice graveled, but he got the words out.

Her eyes searched his. "I was so afraid. I was afraid I wouldn't see you again. That I wouldn't..."

Another tear trailed down, and she looked so vulnerable and honest and beautiful.

He pulled her to him, wrapping his arms around her, and she buried her face against his chest. Her forehead fit in the hollow of his neck so perfectly, as if she were meant to be right there. Was she trembling? He stroked her hair. "It's all right, my love. We're safe. Both of us."

This. This was what he'd needed ever since he'd seen that monster choking her. His arms around her, breathing in her scent, burying his face in her rich auburn hair.

She was home. No matter what burned to the ground or was stripped away from him, as long as he could wrap his arms around Patsy, he would be fine. And she was opening her heart to the Lord, seeing Him work for her good.

Thank You, Father.

No matter what Jonah had lost last night, with this woman in his arms, all was right in his world.

* * *

*T*ears pricked Patience's eyes as Jonah held her close. This was exactly what she'd needed, what she'd longed for. His arms around her, the comfort of his strength.

Ever since she'd first spotted that man last night, she'd craved the safety of Jonah's presence.

But as much as she wanted to, she couldn't stay like this forever. They had to face the reality of Jonah's destroyed cabin.

She forced herself to ease back, then glanced down the trail toward the ruins of his cabin. "What will you do now? With the cabin, I mean."

"I guess we should have a look, see how bad the damage is."

They continued along the path. As they approached the

scorched remnants, Jonah slowed, finally coming to a halt beside her.

The sight must be a punch to the gut. The roof had completely caved in, leaving only charred beams reaching toward the sky like blackened fingers. Most of the walls were gone, too, reduced to piles of rubble. Soot and ash coated everything.

The only things left standing were the stone chimney and the new cast iron cookstove, now hovered like a sad survivor amid the destruction.

Her chest ached for Jonah. All the hours he'd poured into crafting the place into a home, all his hopes for the future, incinerated in a single night.

She wanted to weep for him, for all he'd lost. But he probably needed her strength right now, not her tears, just as he'd been strength for her moments ago. Reaching out, she slipped her cool hand into his large, calloused one. If only there were more she could do to help, to somehow make this devastating blow more bearable.

He squeezed her fingers, his grip almost painful. They stood like that for a long moment, the world silent and still except for the wind sighing through the trees.

Finally, Jonah let out a heavy breath, his broad shoulders sagging. "Guess there's not much that can be saved."

Her heart twisted at the weariness and resignation in his tone. She understood what it meant to lose everything, to start over. She'd done that once before.

"Will you rebuild here?" She spoke the question softly.

Jonah faced her, his blue eyes searching hers with an intensity that made her breath catch. The air between them seemed to thicken, heavy with unspoken words and emotions.

"What is it?" she finally whispered, unable to bear the tension.

He cradled her face, his thumb skimming across her cheekbone. "I'm not sure if it's too soon to say this..."

Her middle churned as worry slipped in. "Please, just be open with me. I want to know what you're thinking, no matter what it is."

He let out a slow exhale, and his eyes softened. "All through the night, I've been wondering if maybe the cabin burning down was a hidden blessing. I started building back when I thought I'd marry Naomi. But after she broke things off, it became a reminder of everything I'd lost, a symbol of the bitterness and loneliness that consumed me."

Pain crossed his face, and the weight in her chest pressed so hard that she could barely draw air. She knew exactly what he meant—all too well.

His gaze turned earnest again. "It wasn't fair of me to ask you to join me here one day. Not in a place with roots tangled in that old pain. You deserve so much more, Patsy. Something built just for you, for us."

Oh.

He was talking about her living here, with him. Which...of course she'd known, maybe, someday... He was courting her. Even so, to dream of it, to hope for it...

They were pale comparisons to what was happening now, with this man looking at her like he was. Wanting her like he did, like she didn't deserve.

Tears blurred her vision. Jonah was too good. Didn't he remember where he'd met her? Didn't he remember the saloon? The...ugliness of her?

His voice turned rough with emotion. "I'm going to court you proper. I'll give you all the time you need. But I fully intend to make you my wife, if you'll have me." The love in his gaze took her breath and any words she might have managed. "And you don't have to give up your dreams to be with me. Now that I'm not tied to this ill-fated place, we can find a new home. Our life, together, can be anywhere we choose."

He lifted her hand to his mouth and pressed a kiss to the back of it. "Whatever you want, wherever that takes us, I'll move heaven and earth to make it happen. Your happiness is what matters most to me."

A sob caught in her throat. How was it possible that this incredible man had come into her life? That he could be so self-less, so willing to put her first?

"Jonah." She choked out his name, then inhaled a breath so she could speak clearly. "All I ever wanted was a home of my own. A safe haven where I wouldn't have to worry about living up to other people's expectations. All I wanted was the freedom to be...me. To not be perfect."

"But you are perfect—for me." Jonah kissed her forehead, the corner of her eye. "Perfectly beautiful and perfectly human and...I wouldn't change anything."

His words made her chest swell almost to bursting. She lifted her palm to his rough jaw. "I thought I needed a pretty white cottage in a green meadow to be happy. But I was wrong. I found my home in you, Jonah. God brought Anna here, and he sent you to find me and bring me to this place. I don't need anything else. Just the two of us together. And Him."

"Patsy." Jonah's voice was rough with emotion. The love in his eyes was so intense, so rich, that her knees went weak. He drew her into his arms, cradling her against his warm chest. She clung to him.

"I don't deserve you." His breath was warm against her hair. "But I'll thank God every day for the rest of my life for bringing you to me."

She tilted her head back, meeting his gaze. The longing in his warm brown eyes reflected of her own. In Jonah, she'd found a future she'd never dared to dream of.

She laid her head on his shoulder, and the rest of the world fell away. The burned-out cabin, the uncertain future, the hardships in their pasts—none of it mattered.

For the first time in her life, Patience knew with absolute certainty that she was exactly where she was meant to be, in the arms of the man she loved, the man who loved her in return. The man who would stand by her side, no matter what challenges lay ahead. A man whose God she knew she could trust.

Here with Jonah, she was home.

CHAPTER 19

*J*onah had to fight to hold his grin as he entered the cabin that night. He'd been riding all afternoon with Patsy, showing her around the ranch. She'd wanted to see every corner, like she actually wanted their home to be somewhere close by. He'd happily go to Wyoming or Colorado if she wanted—or back to Boston, where she grew up. But building their life near his family would be pretty near perfect, if that was truly what she wanted.

Dinah carried a plate of cookies to the table. "We already finished dinner, but you and Patience can fill plates from the pot on the stove. We're having cookies now. Where *is* Patience?" She raised her brows at him.

"Washing her hands at the water wagon. She'll be in shortly."

The rest of his brothers sat around the table, even Sampson, though he slumped back in his chair. His face was still pale and drawn, but at least he'd made it out of bed.

Jonah took his seat and reached for a cookie. He could eat the meal with Patience once she came in.

Jericho clasped his hands on the table in front of him. "I

think a few of us need to go to Helena and track down this Mick character."

Jonah's middle tightened. His big brother sure had a way of knocking the joy out of a fellow. He couldn't stay in the happy daze of courtship when danger still lurked, ready to strike at their family again.

Sampson shook his head. "We shouldn't mess with Mick. You don't know what he's capable of."

"All the more reason to confront him." Jericho's jaw was set, never a good sign if you wanted to change his mind. "We can't let him think he can threaten us without consequences."

Jude nodded slowly. "I agree with Jericho. If we don't take action, Mick will only grow bolder." A hint of pain creased the corners of his eyes. "He's already stolen nearly a year's worth of strawberries—of hard work. We can't let him take what few crates are left in the shed."

Jude probably felt this hit the worst. It was thanks to his hard work and oversight that they'd had so many crates of shined and packed sapphires in the first place. It sounded like he'd given up on getting them back.

They *had* to go after this Mick fellow and take back what had been stolen.

Yet, every time he thought about riding with his brothers to Helena, his spirit churned. *Is this You, God? Are You telling me to stay here?*

In typical Jericho-style, he ignored his brothers' protests and comments. "Jonah and Jude, you'll ride with me to find out the lay of the land. If we can get the sapphires back right away, we will." His gaze shifted to the younger brothers. "If we need more help, one of us will come back for the rest of you. Maybe Two Stones too."

That last part was a good idea. Their good friend and closest neighbor would be glad to help. Maybe he could even go in Jonah's place...

"I'd like to go too. I can help." Gil leaned forward, determination sobering his expression.

Jericho squinted, studying the younger brother, probably torn between his instinct to protect him and his desire to have another gun at his side. His gaze flicked to Jonah as if he was asking for his input.

Jonah gave a slight nod. "Gil can go in my place."

"All right." Jericho's tone weighed heavy with resignation. "Gil, you can come with Jude and me. Today's Friday and we'll need a day to get things ready. Let's leave Monday at first light."

He turned to Jonah and raised one brow. "And you, little brother..." Jonah braced himself for what his brother might say. Maybe something like, *See if you can keep from burning the outhouse down.* "I know I can count on you to keep everyone here safe."

Jonah froze, then studied Jericho's face. Had he really meant that? Not as a joke but in earnest?

Jericho gave a nod, then pushed back from the table.

His brothers chuckled, and as they dispersed for their evening chores, Patsy stepped into the cabin. His heart swelled at the sight of her.

Gil was headed outside and tipped his hat as he passed her. "Evening, Miss Patsy."

The wink he sent Jonah did nothing to squelch his pleasure at her presence. He'd endure any amount of ribbing from his brothers if it meant he got to spend the rest of his life with this woman by his side.

* * *

*P*atsy breathed in the crisp mountain air as she rode beside Jonah down the winding mountain trail. Today was cooler than it had been in recent days, the scent of pine and damp earth filling her lungs. She'd asked Jonah to show her every part of this ranch so she could get to know what she'd begun to pray would one day be her permanent home. This was their second day riding. Today, Jonah was taking her to the south pasture.

As they emerged from the shadowed tree line and the landscape stretched out before her, the view made her suck in a breath and rein in her gelding so she could take it all in.

The valley stretched out like a lush green carpet, dotted with wildflowers that swayed in the breeze. A sparkling stream meandered through the center, its gentle babbling carried on the wind. Her heart ached with a sense of belonging, as if this land had been waiting for her arrival.

Jonah pulled up beside her. "Something wrong?"

She shook her head, her heart almost too full for words. "Nothing's wrong. It's just...this is it. Just like the painting. This is exactly what I wanted. My dream." She motioned to the valley before them. "There's the green grass, the creek running through it." She pointed to a spot on the left. "And that's where the little white cottage would go. Can't you just picture it?"

She almost couldn't breathe as she turned back to him. Would he realize how important this was? A valley this large must be precious pasture land. In fact, a herd of cattle grazed on the far end, black dots in the distance. And maybe he didn't want to be this far from his family. The ride down the mountain had taken nearly an hour. Jude and Angela's cabin was less than a five-minute walk to the main house and barn. Naomi and Eric's too.

But Jonah's expression had turned soft, his eyes smiling. "This is what you want? Are you sure?"

She nodded, tears stinging her eyes. This felt too wonderful to be real.

On the trip back from Fort Benton, she'd made peace with the idea that she could be happy in a life that looked different than what she'd planned. She'd talked with Naomi and Eric, then they'd all talked with Anna. For now, her niece would continue to live with them. Anna needed all the love they surrounded her with. And Patsy would still be part of her life—a daily part. This felt right, finally.

Especially now that she'd finally accepted Jonah and his self-less love, the welcoming circle of his family, and the God who'd proved that He saw her, that He cared, and that He would answer when she cried out to Him...all of these were more than enough to fill her with joy and contentment. To give her a life even better than she'd dreamed of.

She gazed at the meadow before her, amazed.

It seemed too much that she could have all of those wonderful things *and* the best parts of her lifelong dream. Only God could have put these pieces together in such a perfect way.

She no longer wanted to live in the cottage alone and inde-pendent. That sounded quite miserable after experiencing the love of the man beside her. As she turned to meet his gaze, the love in his eyes made the tears fall once more. Happy tears. Tears that overflowed from so much joy she couldn't contain it.

Jonah must have understood, for he reached for her hand, slipping his strong, work-roughened palm against her softer one. She soaked in the feeling of protection that always came from even this simple touch.

Together, she and Jonah could accomplish their dreams—her little white cottage, his cabin filled with love and laughter.

Together, they would heal, grow, and build a life and a family she would treasure with every passing day.

* * *

I pray you loved Jonah and Patsy's story!

Gil finally gets his story in the next book in the series, and what a surprise he's in for as he searches for Sampson and the stolen sapphires...

Turn the page for a sneak peek of *Pretending to be the Mountain Man's Wife,* the next book in the Brothers of Sapphire Ranch series!

- Pretend Marriage
- Secret Baby
- Opposites Attract
- So much more!

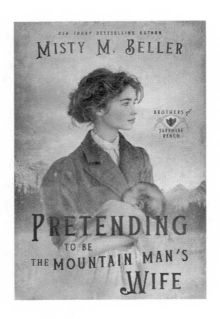

SNEAK PEEK: PRETENDING TO BE THE MOUNTAIN MAN'S WIFE

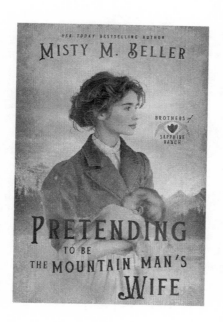

Determined to find his missing brother and catch the elusive mastermind behind the theft of his family's precious sapphires, Gil Coulter embarks on a solo mission to the remote town where the criminal is rumored to reside. As Gil scours the surrounding wilderness for *the thief's hidden lair, he crosses paths with a captivating young woman who harbors secrets of her own.*

Jess McPharland has spent her life hidden in the mountains, doing her best to stay separate from her family's business. Yet the secret she's just discovered will change her life forever. She offers a silent prayer, pleading for a man to help her conceal the truth she's only just discovered. As if in answer, Gil Coulter rides through the trees, seeking the very criminal Jess calls Father. Now she must find a way to ask this stranger for the ultimate favor—to pose as her husband and shield her from the consequences of a change she won't be able to hide much longer.

As Gil and Jess navigate the treacherous landscape and the greater danger from her father and his cronies, they find themselves caught in a web of danger, deception, and unexpected attraction. With each passing moment, the stakes grow higher, and the line between pretense and truth blurs. Will the love growing between them be enough to protect Jess's secret and lead them to the justice Gil seeks, or will the truth shatter everything they've risked their lives to build?

Get <u>PRETENDING TO BE THE MOUNTAIN MAN'S WIFE</u>, <u>the next book in the Brothers of Sapphire Ranch series, at your</u> <u>favorite retailer!</u>

Did you enjoy Jonah and Patsy's story? I hope so!
Would you take a quick minute to leave a review where you purchased the book?
It doesn't have to be long. Just a sentence or two telling what you liked about the story!

* * *

To receive a free book and get updates when new Misty M. Beller books release, go to https://mistymbeller.com/freebook

ALSO BY MISTY M. BELLER

Brothers of Sapphire Ranch

Healing the Mountain Man's Heart

Marrying the Mountain Man's Best Friend

Protecting the Mountain Man's Treasure

Earning the Mountain Man's Trust

Winning the Mountain Man's Love

Pretending to be the Mountain Man's Wife

Sisters of the Rockies

Rocky Mountain Rendezvous

Rocky Mountain Promise

Rocky Mountain Journey

The Mountain Series

The Lady and the Mountain Man

The Lady and the Mountain Doctor

The Lady and the Mountain Fire

The Lady and the Mountain Promise

The Lady and the Mountain Call

This Treacherous Journey

This Wilderness Journey

This Freedom Journey (novella)

This Courageous Journey

This Homeward Journey

This Daring Journey

This Healing Journey

Call of the Rockies

Freedom in the Mountain Wind

Hope in the Mountain River

Light in the Mountain Sky

Courage in the Mountain Wilderness

Faith in the Mountain Valley

Honor in the Mountain Refuge

Peace in the Mountain Haven

Grace on the Mountain Trail

Calm in the Mountain Storm

Joy on the Mountain Peak

Brides of Laurent

A Warrior's Heart

A Healer's Promise

A Daughter's Courage

Hearts of Montana

Hope's Highest Mountain

Love's Mountain Quest

Faith's Mountain Home

Honor's Mountain Promise

Texas Rancher Trilogy

The Rancher Takes a Cook

The Ranger Takes a Bride

The Rancher Takes a Cowgirl

Wyoming Mountain Tales